LIZ FIELDING

THE BRIDESMAID'S ROYAL BODYGUARD

Complete and Unabridged

LINFORD
Leicester

First published in Great Britain in 2017

First Linford Edition
published 2018

A catalogue record for this book is available
from the British Library.

ISBN 978–1–4448–3904–3

Published by
F. A. Thorpe (Publishing)
Anstey, Leicestershire

Set by Words & Graphics Ltd.
Anstey, Leicestershire
Printed and bound in Great Britain by
T. J. International Ltd., Padstow, Cornwall

This book is printed on acid-free paper

Once in a while,
right in the middle of an ordinary life,
love gives us a fairy tale.

Becoming a Princess

1

'Ally!'

Ally Parker glanced at the clock and sighed. Jennifer Harmon, the landlady of the Three Bells and her temporary boss, never failed to find a last-minute job that would take her over her basic hours. Extra minutes for which she would not be paid.

Mostly, because she needed a job — even one that involved scrubbing the floors of a busy gastropub — she gritted her teeth and got on with it, but not today.

She had to get away promptly for the first test in the once-in-a-lifetime PR gig handed her by her BFF, Hope Kennard. Not that she could tell Jennifer the reason she had to leave on time.

Much as she'd enjoy wiping the superior look off Jennifer's face by explaining that she was meeting Count Fredrik

Jensson, Head of Security for the San Michele royal family, this morning at Hasebury Hall, Hope's marriage to His Serene Highness Prince Jonas Reval was very much on a need-to-know basis. Family, bridesmaids . . .

'Ally!' The second summons was sung out so sweetly that she knew Pete must have joined his wife in the bar to set up for the lunchtime rush. That would make things easier, at least for today. Jennifer would dissect any excuse she offered with her scalpel of a tongue but Pete would wave her out of the door. It would give his wife even more reason to give her a hard time when he wasn't around but right now she'd take it.

She gave the range of stainless steel sinks one last wipe down but kept on her pink rubber gloves when she walked into the bar so that she couldn't be accused of not working every second she was being paid for.

'Oh, there you are, Ally. I was beginning to think you'd slipped away early.'

Jennifer looked her up and down, clearly enjoying the fact that, having lost her 'glamorous' job in London, her working wardrobe now consisted of a wrap-around pinny that had belonged to her grandmother and the scarf she wrapped around her hair to protect it from the scent of cooking and ale that lingered in the air.

'No, still here — ' she looked up as the bar clock clicked onto the hour, setting her free ' — although I do have to leave promptly today,' she reminded her, pulling off one of the gloves to emphasize the point.

'Of course, my dear. I wouldn't dream of keeping you a minute over your hours.' Her smile might have convinced anyone who didn't have the misfortune to work for her. 'The only reason I called is because you have a visitor.'

A visitor?

She turned as Jennifer gestured in the direction of a tall figure standing with his back to her in front of the fire.

Who . . . ?

He turned as if she'd spoken the word out loud and any number of words skittered through her brain — mostly of the what-the-hell variety — but her overriding thought was that Count Fredrik Jensson looked a lot more dangerous in person than he had in the photographs she'd found online.

His thick, light brown hair, cut almost brutally short, looked as if it had been touched by the hard frost riming the hedges as she set out for work at dawn. His eyes were a matching icy grey and he had the hard-boned good looks that turned strong women to jelly.

Jennifer, gossip antennae twitching like the whiskers of a mouse scenting cheese, was simpering in expectation of an introduction.

The man might be dangerously sexy but he was also dangerously stupid. Fortunately, her three years working for a gossip magazine had given her plenty of practice in diversionary tactics.

Before he could speak she flung her

arms wide and exclaimed, 'Fredrik!' hoping he'd have the sense to follow her lead. 'How wonderful! I wasn't expecting to see you until later.'

The last, at least, was true. Plan A had been to present herself at Hasebury Hall on the dot of ten o'clock, city-smart and thoroughly professional in her 'serious' suit and the Manolos she'd bought with a bonus when she'd been flavour of the month at *Celebrity* magazine.

She hadn't anticipated the need for a Plan B but no one could accuse her of being slow on her feet.

Jennifer, agog at the arrival of a drop-dead gorgeous male, needed distracting. If she thought they had history, she wouldn't be wondering what he was doing in Combe St Philip; her imagination would already be filling in the blanks.

Peeling off her other glove and stuffing them both in her apron pocket, Ally placed her hands on the sleeves of his coat and, leaning forward to brush her lips against his cold cheek, murmured, 'Just play along.'

For a heartbeat nothing happened, but Count Fredrik Jensson was not slow on his feet, either. While she was distracted by the enticing scent of cold skin, tingly fresh air, leaves mouldering beneath the bare canopy of winter woods, his hands encircled her waist and before she could blink he was crushing her against the soft cashmere of his coat and the hard body it concealed.

'Alice . . . '

Never had her name sounded so desirable and, held by his penetrating grey stare, she only realized his intention a split second before he lowered his mouth to hers.

Her tiny mew of protest was obliterated by the touch of cold lips that sent a shiver to her toes. Her brain, seeking an appropriate response to the shocking experience of being kissed senseless by a man she'd only moments before set eyes on, floundered as the ice of his mouth combined with the heat of hers in an explosion of pleasure.

Her last coherent thought as she closed her eyes and kissed him back was *more* . . .

'Hey, get a room, you two!'

Shamefully, it was the Count who responded first, his eyes giving nothing away as he lifted his head. In an attempt to retrieve a little self-respect Ally staggered back and would have stumbled if he hadn't been holding her.

Her breath hitched in her throat as, still reeling from her response, she clung to him. Her cheeks were on fire; his, in contrast, were pale, his eyes glacier cold but she wasn't fooled by the surface ice; beneath the frozen exterior there lay a hidden volcano.

Dangerous . . .

'Hi,' she finally managed, when the silence had gone on too long. 'What a wonderful surprise. I d-didn't expect to see you — ' her voice was shaky but under the circumstances any woman's voice would shake ' — until later.'

He laid his hand against her cheek as if to cool it. 'I'm an impatient man,' he murmured softly in a seductively accented voice and her knees sent up a plea for reinforcement. 'I couldn't wait.' He rescued a wayward strand of hair that had escaped as her scarf slipped back and tucked it behind her ear, holding it there, his fingers chill against her neck. 'I apologize if my arrival is ill-timed.'

Ill-timed was putting it mildly. She grabbed at the thought, anything to distract from the tingle of awareness lit by his kiss. The let's-do-it-again dance of hormones straining at the leash like an excited puppy.

The San Michele royal family weren't exactly thrilled by their youngest son's choice of bride and even less happy that she'd insisted on being married from her family home. It certainly wasn't going to do Hope's cause any good if they discovered that the woman she'd chosen to handle her personal PR was moonlighting as a cleaner in the village pub.

But Fredrik wasn't apologizing to her. He was looking at Jennifer.

'Not at all,' she replied, with the satisfied smile of a woman whose currency was gossip. Taking in every detail of this unexpected gift. 'Can I get you a cup of coffee while you're waiting, Mr . . . ?' She paused expectantly — she had his first name but wanted more.

Ally, snapping out of a lustful haze, cut in before he could fill the gap and, finally getting her knees under control, stepped away.

'Thank you, Jennifer, but we'll have one at home.'

She shrugged. 'Another time.' Then, almost as an after-thought: 'Is there any chance you could come in an hour earlier tomorrow, Ally? We've a coach party booked for lunch and we're short-handed so I need someone to set up the dining room.'

Jennifer would rather have done it herself than give her extra hours but no doubt it amused the wretched woman to think she would be dragging her out of the warm arms of a lover and into a cold dawn.

Let her think it. An extra hour, even at minimum wages, would be very welcome.

'Happy to help,' she said, absently, looking up at the Count with what she hoped was a suitably sappy expression but there was nothing faked about the huskiness in her voice as she added, right on cue. 'It's quicker if we go out the back way.'

'Goodbye, Fredrik,' Jennifer called as they made their way to the rear of the pub. 'I hope to see you again.'

He stopped in the doorway, turned, forcing her to wait while he acknowledged Jennifer with a formal nod of his head. 'Madam.'

Polite, noncommittal, very foreign.

She swallowed a groan. News of his arrival would be the talk of the village by teatime but at least no one would be speculating on his reason for being in Combe St Philip.

The wedding was tightly under wraps and her entire future depended on keeping it that way. The first hint of it in the gossip mags before the official announcement from the royal palace and everyone would be looking at her.

'Not a word until we're outside,' she hissed, using the excuse of grabbing her coat to let go of his arm.

She didn't stop to put it on but once they were outside in the car park he took it from her and held it so that she could slip her arms in the sleeves, holding it in place for a moment, his hands on her shoulders.

It would have looked good to anyone watching from the pub but a shiver went through her at the memory of other hands on her shoulders in this car park. She knew it wasn't the same. The sun was shining, Fredrik Jensson was merely playing along with the charade she'd begun, but she stepped away and turned on him.

'What on earth were you thinking?'

His eyebrows rose the merest fraction

but it was enough to warn her that she was over-reacting.

The sensible response would be amusement, maybe mixed with a little embarrassment at the situation they'd found themselves in but there had been a rawness about that kiss, an intensity about Fredrik Jensson that unnerved her, making her unusually jumpy.

Unlike Fredrik Jensson.

If he felt any remorse or embarrassment for the scene he'd caused, there was no indication of it. His mouth might be made for sin but his face was made for poker.

'My time is limited. I don't have time to waste waiting for you.'

The way he said 'you', told her everything she needed to know. The San Michele royal family might be unhappy with Prince Jonas's choice of bride, but nowhere near as unhappy as Count Fredrik Jensson was with her own involvement in the wedding.

He'd undoubtedly checked her out — it was his job and she didn't blame him for that — but he couldn't have made it plainer that he hadn't liked what he'd found. Well, he wasn't her idea of Prince Charming either but they had to work together like it or not. Not, however, before she put him straight.

'I wasn't keeping you waiting to be annoying. I was working. I'm thrilled to help Hope with the local PR for her wedding but I have bills to pay.'

'I'm sure your consultancy fee is more than generous.'

'When a friend needs help, you don't produce a price list.' She had no doubt that her connection to the royal wedding would bring in job offers but she was done with the 'gossip' business. 'How did you find me?'

In the bright sunshine, the ice grey of his eyes had the sparkle of granite. There was the same hardness about him and yet his mouth had softened as he'd kissed her, evoking a response that had left her wanting more.

As if he had the same thought he turned abruptly away. 'I asked Max

Kennard where you lived. Your mother invited me to wait for you but . . . '
Another shrug, this time leaving her to draw her own conclusions.

'You escaped?' She had no doubt her mother had tempted him with offers of coffee and home-made cake in order to give him the third degree and without warning she was struggling to keep a straight face. Hysteria . . . She cleared her throat. 'Impressive.'

The bad news was that while he had escaped a grilling from her mother, she had nowhere to hide and would have to come up with something convincing by the time she reached home. News of that scene in the Three Bells would be all around the village by teatime and it would be cruel to leave her mother hanging out to dry when the phone calls started.

'I assumed your first security concern would be the grounds of Hasebury Hall,' she said, when he didn't answer.

'They are,' he replied. 'I walked them at first light.'

Of course he had. He was an impatient man, not given to wasting time hanging around for the likes of her. It accounted for the rich, peaty scent of leaf mould . . .

'Good decision,' she said quickly. The last thing she should be thinking about was the woodland scent that clung to him. 'The gardens are magical with everything frosted over. The whole world seems to turn pink as the sun rises.'

'I was more concerned with the lack of secure boundaries,' he replied.

Philistine . . .

'It would have been a lot tougher before most of the estate was sold off.' She glanced up at him. 'The royal family aren't under threat, are they?' She paused as they reached the Market Cross where their ways diverged. 'I thought San Michele was peaceful.'

He shrugged. 'No country is immune from hotheads. Those who want to make the front page for whatever cause they're espousing. And it isn't just

Hasebury Hall, or Combe St Philip. The royal family and their staff will be staying at Westonbury Court when they are here for the wedding.'

'Westonbury?'

'The family have connections there.'

'Well that's handy,' she said, making a mental note of this unexpected nugget of information. Her mother knew the housekeeper and with luck she could blag a tour of the house. Not that she was going to tell him that. 'You'll be liaising with the Chief Constable about security, I imagine.'

'I'll make contact, let him know that the royal party will be at Westonbury this summer. The reason for their stay will keep until the palace makes the official announcement. This visit is simply to reconnoitre the area, uncover potential problems and prepare a security plan.'

'Right.'

It was like talking to wood, she thought. She was doing her best but apart from that kiss, not much was coming back, which was probably a Good Thing. The kiss had been more than enough . . .

'I've prepared a file for you with the contact details of everyone who will be involved locally and I've included a large scale map of the village and the surrounding area.' She didn't wait for his thanks. 'I'll, um, dash home for a shower and change and meet you back at the Hall.'

There was little point going ahead with her plan to impress her first official contact with San Michele. He'd seen her at her worst and glamming it up with her London career-girl image would just make those expressive eyebrows lift at her attempt to impress him.

About to head off up the lane she was struck by a terrible thought and turned back to face him.

'You didn't mention your reason for being in Combe St Philip when you spoke to my mother? She doesn't know about the wedding.'

'You haven't told her that you are going to be a royal bridesmaid?' He sounded surprised.

'The news will keep until after the official announcement,' she said, parroting him. A crease appeared at the corner of his mouth. The first suggestion of a smile? Or was it just an irritated twitch that someone who had worked for a gossip magazine could keep a secret.

'I asked for you,' he said. 'Nothing more.'

'And she told you where I was? Just like that?' she persisted. 'She didn't grill you for every detail about who you were, where you'd come from, why you were looking for me?'

'She may have asked. I didn't feel the need to answer,' he replied with the look of a man who never had to explain himself.

'Again, impressive!' she said, unable to resist a grin.

Fredric Jensson did not appear to think it was amusing and actually it wasn't. Her mother would have had time to fine-tune the third degree by now and wouldn't be so easily put off. Fortunately, she had anticipated the need for a story to cover her meetings with the Count but it was going to need a few tweaks.

'Since we needed a story to cover your presence in Combe St Philip,' she said, 'I thought we could say that Hope and I met you at a party in London. You were planning to visit the Cotswolds on business and Hope invited you to stay at the Hall. She's in London, up to her eyes in work right now, so you get me as your local guide.'

He frowned. 'Who will be interested?'

'Are you kidding? Any stranger staying at the Hall will give the village something to talk about. By tomorrow there would have been speculation about you and Hope. Walking into the Three Bells looking for me scuppered that line of gossip. Instead of marrying Hope you'll be sleeping with me.'

'An interesting distinction,' he said,

'but hardly surprising in view of your enthusiastic welcome.'

A smile — even half a smile — would have taken the edge off that.

'I'm so sorry,' she said, getting a little tired of his attitude. 'Should I have bobbed a curtsey and said, 'Count Fredrik Jensson, what an honour to meet you?'' The crease made another appearance but she'd given up on the smile. He was doubtless clenching his jaw, irritated that a common village wench was prepared to speak her mind. 'I thought this was supposed to be a low-profile visit. You were the one who turned it into something else.'

There was an endless moment of silence. The only movement was his breath misting the frozen air and Ally, afraid that she'd gone too far, held her own breath.

'I only use the title on ceremonial occasions — ' his icy control was unnerving ' — and save your curtsies for their serene highnesses. They will expect it.'

'Don't worry,' she replied, 'I've been

practising.' A rare attack of nerves meant that had come out rather more flippantly than she'd intended.

Count Fredrik's jaw tightened noticeably.

'You may think it's an antiquated formality, Miss Parker, but the San Michele court is governed by strict protocol. When your mother told me that you had a job at the Three Bells, it didn't occur to me that you would be scrubbing the kitchen floor. You'd better hope their highnesses don't find out.'

Her own jaw tightened in response. It wasn't a glamorous job. She was no longer visiting celebrities in their homes, persuading them to open their hearts and closets for the weekly gratification of *Celebrity*'s readers, but it was honest work and she wasn't ashamed of it.

'What did you think I'd be doing?' she asked. 'The Three Bells doesn't serve breakfast and I don't usually start on the gin until the sun is over the yard arm.' She gave him back the glacial stare. 'Today might yet prove an exception.'

'Your mother did try very hard to persuade me to wait for you,' he admitted, running a hand over his hair and looking a touch discomforted, 'but I misunderstood her motives.'

She doubted that. A good-looking man turning up out of the blue and asking for her would have given her mother all kinds of ideas. The big white dress, grandchildren . . .

He was fortunate that she hadn't dragged him in over the threshold by his expensive lapels.

'When she finally explained that you were working at the Three Bells, I assumed it was as a PR consultant. I had planned to have a cup of coffee while waiting for you.'

'Oh.'

'It is what you do?' he pressed.

'When I'm not scrubbing floors?'

Stop it . . .

She forced herself to relax, smile.

'I'm a journalist, not a PR consultant. I'm doing it this once for Hope,' she said. 'No one else.'

2

Count Fredrik Jensson looked confused.

'To be honest,' she said, 'the pub could do with a brand makeover but while Pete would be up for it, Jennifer would rather stick pins in her eyes than give me the job.'

'Why?'

Because, Ally thought, her adorable, but clueless mother had bragged endlessly about her job on the international gossip magazine, *Celebrity*. Who she'd met, where she'd been.

'It's a long story.'

Sacked on the spot for an incident that had made her a laughing stock, unemployable by any gossip magazine, no longer able to pay her portion of the flat share, and with some eye-watering credit card bills that had been manageable when she'd had a regular income, she'd returned home to rethink her career options. Meanwhile she'd taken whatever job was going.

There had not been much to choose from apart from cleaning at the pub and serving lunch to the tourists at the Old Forge, which had evoked a certain amount of *Schadenfreude* in all those who'd been forced to listen to her mother for the last couple of years. Jennifer took enormous pleasure in giving her the most menial jobs she could find.

She'd been grinning and bearing it when Hope had shared the thrilling news that she was marrying San Michele's Prince Jonas and had rejected the brouhaha of a cathedral wedding and palace reception. She wanted a proper village wedding right here in Combe St Philip, and she wanted her and Flora Deare — the third in their BFF triumvirate — as bridesmaids.

'But you're handling the PR side of things for Hope?'

She glanced at him. 'Actually, not so

much her — she's keeping her head down, working in London.' She had his attention now. 'Sir Max Kennard, unlike his father, is a quiet, reserved man. He's agreed to hold the wedding at Hasebury Hall because he feels he owes Hope that, but I imagine even a scaled down 'ordinary' royal wedding is pretty much his worst nightmare.' Quite how 'ordinary' the wedding would be with a host of royals descending on the village was a moot point. 'Hope wants me to protect him from the worst of it.'

'And you think you can handle that?'

Good question.

It might not be a British prince who was marrying the local girl but without a home-grown royal wedding to fill their pages, the media would go overboard for Hope and Jonas. Combe St Philip would be swarming with journalists and television news crews, all of them wanting background on the local girl who was marrying a prince.

'It's all about preparation,' she assured him. 'I'm working on a press pack.

A potted history of the village and the Kennard family, a relaxed portrait of Hope, a few lines about how they'd met.' Give them enough to fill their column inches, provide them with good quality pictures and a few quotes and most of them would be satisfied.

There was, after all, nothing like a royal wedding to sell papers.

And then there was the village. There was no escaping the fact that Hope's idiot of a father — having been duped by 'friends' into some dodgy financial scheme — had died in prison; not everyone was going to be overjoyed for her.

Part of her job would be to keep everyone focused on the upside of the royal wedding taking place in Combe St Philip. The huge financial boost from which everyone would benefit. Including Jennifer 'sourface' Harmon.

Meanwhile Fredrik Jensson's default setting was caution. It went with the job and she didn't blame him for that. Obviously he'd run a check on everyone involved, knew her history, knew that she'd lost her job. He probably knew to the last penny how much she owed on her credit cards.

'Hope chose me because she trusts me,' she said. About to add that she would never betray her, she let it go. Nothing she said would convince him that she wasn't about to sell the royal secrets for hard cash. She just had to get on with the job, be herself and let events prove him wrong. 'Our problem now is how to handle the fallout from what happened back there in the bar.'

'Fallout?'

'This is a small village. Your presence will already have been remarked, questions asked. Who are you? Where have you come from? What are you doing here?'

'It's none of their business.'

'Of course not. Which makes it all the more interesting.' She stopped, looked at him. 'I suppose if there's going to be speculation about your presence at Hasebury Hall, it's better the gossip is about me rather than Hope.'

He had taken a step beyond her and turned to look at her. 'You? Surely you mean us?' He didn't look thrilled at the prospect.

Of course she meant '*us*'. If he hadn't got carried away . . . If she hadn't responded with quite so much enthusiasm . . .

'I'm sorry if it bothers you but it's what they'll think anyway, so we might as well use it to our advantage. Maybe, if you think of it as a security measure, it will be easier to bear.' Enough. Before he could say anything else to irritate her, she held out her hand. 'We appear to have got off on the wrong foot, Count. Shall we try again? How d'you do, Count Fredrik Jensson. Welcome to Combe St Philip.'

There was a long moment before he reached out and enveloped her hand in his.

'Thank you, Miss Parker.'

It was the moment to let out the breath she was holding but she seemed to have lost control of her breathing in that moment he'd turned and looked at her. She'd been struggling for it ever since he'd kissed her.

Breathe . . .

Do not think about the kiss.

'Under the circumstances . . . ' Her throat was thick and the words came out as little more than a whisper. She cleared it, tried again. 'Under the circumstances, I think people will find such formality a little odd,' she finally managed. 'My friends call me Ally.' When he didn't respond, she added, 'What do people usually call you?'

'Sir.'

The smile froze on her lips.

'However, if we are going to cause a scandal,' he continued, 'Fredrik would be more appropriate.'

There was nothing in his expression to tell her if he was teasing.

A car came down the hill and Ally stepped aside without taking her eyes off Fredrik Jensson.

'Yes . . . ' She cleared her throat,

again, trying hard not to think about what creating a scandal with him would involve. What his hard, calloused hands would feel like against her skin. What his mouth would feel like . . . 'Fredrik.' His name was little more than a husky puff of frosted air. 'I go this way. I'll, um, catch up with you at the Hall.'

'That's just a waste of time.' And he was an impatient man. The thought sent a ripple of anticipation skittering up her spine. 'Does your mother make a decent cup of coffee?'

Decent?

It was a perfectly ordinary word and she wasn't in the habit of breaking out in shivery lust at the drop of a hat. At all. Ever. She could flirt with the best of them but found it easy to keep an arm's length between herself and anyone who wanted to take it further.

He was waiting for an answer.

Coffee . . .

She was tempted to tell him that her mother — who prided herself on her crema — used the cheapest instant from the village shop in order to give herself a little breathing space, a moment to recover from the impact of his presence, that kiss, but she couldn't bring herself to tell such an outrageous lie.

Hoping that he was a coffee snob she managed a discouraging, 'Not bad.'

'Not bad will do.' Accurately reading her dismay, he came closer to a smile than anything she'd seen so far. 'I was a soldier. Hot and strong was the best I could hope for.'

Hot and strong . . .

He didn't wait for her answer but set off in the direction of her parents' cottage, favouring one leg. From everything she'd read, he'd been lucky to keep the other and she suspected the scars were not just the ones left by the mortar shell. Considering what he'd lost it was scarcely any wonder that he was a grouch. A very hot grouch . . .

'Oh, pull yourself together, Ally,' she muttered.

Handling the local PR for Hope's

royal wedding had given her the chance to reboot her career and she wasn't about to waste it. She'd researched everyone involved in the circus that would descend on Combe St Philip that summer, and she was determined not to put a foot wrong.

Count Fredrik Otto Jensson, having aroused her interest with his public exploits, had proved elusive on the personal front.

His achievements as a mountaineer, his heroics as a soldier, had been well documented but there had been no mention of a wife or family. Even his Scandinavian name was an enigma and the face gazing out of official portraits gave little away.

Up close and personal it was still unreadable.

It shouldn't matter. He wasn't one of the royals, wouldn't feature in the wedding diary she was creating for Hope and Jonas. In the flesh, however, he commanded attention and all those blanks were now raising questions that, after years working on a gossip magazine, came so naturally to her.

Who was Fredrik Jensson? What drove him? What secrets was he keeping locked away behind those cool grey eyes and the hard, straight line of his mouth?

Realizing that he was alone, Fredrik paused and glanced back. Ally Parker hadn't moved, but was standing perfectly still, watching him.

The sun was rising behind her and the fair streaks in her dark plaited hair, ruffled and flying away where she'd pulled off her scarf, were lit up around her head like a halo. An illusion, he knew. Despite a smile that could melt permafrost, it would be a mistake to believe that she was any kind of angel. Her lips had left a warm, velvet-soft imprint on his cold cheek, heated him to the bone with her response to a kiss that should never have happened, but those who worked for gossip magazines had to have hearts of cold, hard stone.

The smile was simply part of the

toolbox: a charm to unlock the secrets of the unwary. As for her lips . . .

Forget her lips; concentrate on what was real.

The first thing he'd done when he'd learned that she was not just a bridesmaid, but would be handling Hope's PR here in Combe St Philip as well, was to run a security check on her. The Net had obliged with dozens of pictures of her interviewing award-clutching celebrities; chatting to minor royals at charity balls; always smiling as she teased out those indiscreet sound-bite quotes from those high on success or champagne. That was all over. She was out of a job, in debt . . .

When he'd raised his concerns, Jonas had brushed them aside. Hope had chosen her and that, apparently, was that.

Since then, she'd managed to con-flate her role into creating a souvenir diary of the wedding preparations that would be published to raise funds for a charitable trust to be established in the name of the new Princess.

She'd asked for access to everyone involved, including the royal family, wanting their thoughts about the wedding, about Hope. While the idea had filled him with horror, he had anticipated a professional, someone with polish and that red-carpet style.

What he'd got was a woman with her hair tied up in a scarf, without a scrap of make-up, living at home with her parents and working as a cleaner in the village pub.

It should have been a complete turn-off, but there was a glow about her that the digitized image had only hinted at and, as she'd reached for him, it had wrapped around him like a hug from a cashmere blanket.

For a moment her smile, her warmth, had immobilized him but then a flash from her green-gold eyes, a demand that he follow her lead, respond to her welcome, had jolted him back to reality. It was an act, a performance for the woman watching from the bar, honed while working for *Celebrity*, and he'd responded with a kiss that he'd intended to be cold, impersonal. His mistake.

Which begged the question: what on earth had happened to her? Why was she working as a cleaner? He'd assumed she'd left *Celebrity* to set up her own PR consultancy but no one would leave a well-paid job without having a solid business plan or, more importantly, having signed up clients in advance.

Clearly she hadn't left voluntarily.

Forget friendship.

Alice Parker and Hope Kennard might have been friends since nursery school but he had to ask himself what a woman reduced to cleaning the local pub would do to climb back on the career ladder.

Realizing that he was waiting, she tucked one of those flyaway strands of hair behind her ear. 'Sorry. I was thinking.' Her breath was a series of distracting little puffs of mist that focused his attention on the soft, luscious lips, naturally pink, sweet as sin . . .

'Should I be worried?'

The smile was back. 'Maybe. I'm sure you've acquainted yourself with Hope's father's fall from grace?'

He grunted an acknowledgement. Prince Jonas's choice of bride had not gone down well in the palace. He had no doubt that the delay in announcing the engagement was down to the vain hope of the Crown Princess that Jonas might yet see sense, forget all this love nonsense and marry the daughter of some aristocratic San Michele family.

Fredrik might be immune to that emotional pitfall, but even he could see it was never going to happen.

'She had a hard time of it for a while at boarding school,' Ally said, turning to look across the honey stone cottages that lay in a curve beneath them. 'And then here in the village.'

'So why have the wedding here?' he asked. 'It would be a great deal easier to hold it in San Michele.'

'No doubt — ' she sounded sympathetic ' — but Combe St Philip is her home.' She looked back at him. He was half a head taller than her but in high heels she would be one of those rare women who could look him in the eye. They would be a perfect fit . . . 'The wedding is an opportunity to put the past behind them, share her joy with people she's known all her life and have a gloriously old-fashioned village wedding.'

That was what Jonas had told him when he'd raised objections to this unconventional venue. He wasn't heir to the throne — the country had had their big royal wedding when his older brother had married. This was Hope's day and if a village wedding was what the woman he'd chosen to spend his life with wanted, a village wedding was what she would have and the rest of them could go hang.

Despite the difficulties it raised, he had admired him for that.

'Is that what you'd choose?' he asked

Ally. A small frown puckered the space between her eyes. 'If the choice was between a great cathedral with half the crowned heads of Europe in attendance or the village church.'

She laughed and the sound rippled around him. 'Not a decision I'm ever going to have to make.'

'It happened to Hope.'

'Hope is special,' she said. 'And lightning doesn't strike in the same place twice.'

'Actually, that's not true.'

'Isn't it?' She shook her head, lifted her shoulders a centimetre or two. 'Who knew.'

'So?'

'I've never thought about it.'

'Not even in your wildest dreams?' he persisted, not sure why he was pressing the issue when he hadn't the slightest interest in the answer.

'Oh . . . ' she said. 'If we're talking wildest dreams that would be Hope and I taking it in turns to wear the Cinderella dress at infant school.

Apparently she was wearing the tiara when the clock struck midnight.'

'Do you envy her?'

'No.' She hadn't hesitated. 'Marriage is tough enough without having everything you do put under the microscope of public opinion.'

'That's something that you would know all about.'

'Yes,' she admitted. 'I've seen what it can do.'

There was no attempt to excuse what she did and he knew that most of the people featured in magazines like *Celebrity* actively courted the publicity because without it they were nothing. Others were paid handsomely to allow exclusive access to their lives, whether they were celebrating the high points or going through some horrendous drama.

'Of course it's easy to be wise before the event,' she said, her smile a little self-mocking now. 'Ask me again when I've met my prince.'

There did not appear to be any candidates. Her invitation to San

Michele would have included a plus-one for the formal dinner and the ball that would follow the official announcement of the engagement. Princess Anna liked a tidy table and didn't want any spare women messing with her plans for Prince Nico, but he hadn't been given a name to check.

'Hope does realize that, once the royal party are seated, there won't be room in the church for the entire village?' he asked, moving the conversation away from the uncomfortably personal.

'Of course. We might have to set up a giant screen on the green although . . . ' They had arrived at her home and she stopped, took a breath. 'Brace yourself,' she said, as she opened the door of her parents' cottage and walked straight in off the lane into a cosy sitting room, warmed by a log fire.

'Mum?' she called. 'I'm home and I've brought Fredrik with me. Can you make him a cup of coffee while I grab a shower?'

Her flustered mother appeared from

the rear of the cottage but, before she could respond, Ally had opened a door and disappeared up the stairs.

* * *

Ally flew up two flights of narrow stairs to her room beneath the eaves, shut the door behind her and, leaning against it, put her hand to her heart as if she could slow its pounding.

Telling herself that it was excitement at the great idea she'd just had that was making her breathless, that it had nothing whatever to do with the arrival of the chiselled-jawed Count Fredrik Jensson, she grabbed some clothes and headed for the bathroom.

Ten minutes later, after the fastest shower in history — she didn't dare leave Fredrik alone with her mother for too long — she was back in the living room. He was sitting, perfectly relaxed, in the armchair beside the fire and it was obvious from her mother's frustrated expression that she'd got nowhere.

'Ally . . . I was just asking Fredrik how he was enjoying his stay in Combe St Philip.'

'He'll be able to tell you more about that when he's actually seen the village, Mum.' She turned to him. 'I help out at the Old Forge café and I'm on the lunch shift today so we should get going.'

She'd abandoned all thought of the smart suit and high heels for a soft check shirt, narrow black corduroy trousers — which she'd tucked into laced-ankle boots — and a brightly coloured hand-knit sweater that had been made by a designer she'd interviewed for a feature in *Celebrity*. She'd fallen in love with it but it had been ridiculously expensive despite a generous discount and she'd been planning to sell it on eBay until Hope had asked her to be involved with the wedding. With luck by the summer her career would be back on track and wearing it today was drawing a line in the sand. The past was behind her and she was totally focused on the future.

'He was asking about the church,' her mother said, a hopeful lift to her voice.

'First stop on our itinerary,' Ally assured her.

'Thank you for the excellent coffee, Mrs Parker.'

Her mother blushed with pleasure at the compliment. 'Debbie, please,' she said, as Ally slipped on her jacket, hooked a tote over her arm and opened the front door so that he could escape. 'I hope we'll see you again soon.'

'Without a doubt,' he replied.

'I'm not sure when I'll be back, Mum,' Ally said, shutting the door behind her, relieved to have got away so easily. 'Did she grill you? I'm afraid that she'll already be on the phone spreading the news about a mysterious stranger staying at the Hall.' His 'without a doubt' would almost certainly have given her ideas.

'In that case we'd better get going before we gather a crowd of sightseers.'

She glanced at him. Was that a

suggestion of humour? There was nothing in his face to suggest amusement but she was beginning to suspect there was more to Fredrik Jensson than his straight face might suggest.

Not a good thing. She had a weakness for men with a wry sense of humour but until this wedding was over she would not, could not, allow herself to be distracted.

3

'Where are all the cars?' Fredrik asked as they walked down through the village.

She followed his gaze along the curve of cottages that stood right against the narrow road leading through the village.

'It's a historic village,' she said. 'The houses are hundreds of years old and listed as ancient monuments. It's regularly used as a location for film and TV.' She reeled off a list of historic films in which Combe St Philip had been used as a location. 'So, no satellite dishes, no PVC replacement windows and definitely no parking.'

'How do the people who live here manage?'

'There are three designated parking areas tucked away out of sight of the visitors. You need a swipe card to access them. Visitors have to use the car park at the top of the hill and walk down.'

'Wedding guests can't be expected to do that,' he pointed out.

'They'll be able to park in the grounds of the Hall.' She patted her tote. 'In the notes I've made for you, I've suggested you ask the Chief Constable to organize a checkpoint at the top of the hill so that invitations can be checked against a guest list.' They had reached the church and not waiting for a response she led the way through the lychgate to the ancient west door of St Philip and All Angels.

Fredrik took a long, slow look around, taking in the frosted grass, steps that led down to an area filled with ancient gravestones and the equally ancient trees that surrounded the churchyard. She had known it all her life but she looked at it now as he must see it: a location full of hiding places.

He turned without a word, pushed open the heavy door and they were immediately enveloped in the hush and scent of seven hundred years of history: old hymn books, incense, nearly a thousand years of people standing, sitting, kneeling to worship that had seeped into the walls.

Dust motes, disturbed by their arrival, danced in the light slanting in through the stained-glass windows and throwing patches of colour onto the white walls. And flanking the arch leading to the choir, the familiar rows of kneeling angels, painted on the wall by someone long forgotten.

'St Philip and All Angels was originally founded in the thirteenth century,' Ally began. 'The nave was added in the fourteenth century and the tower was completed two hundred years later.' Was he listening? She pressed on. 'The stained-glass window featuring the arms of the de la Hase family — ' she pointed to an impressive window on the left-hand side of the church ' — was endowed by Sir Ralph Kennard. A newly made baronet, he married Elizabeth de la Hase, the daughter and only surviving heir of Sir James de la Hase in 1632.'

'How did Sir Ralph get his title?' Fredrik asked. Perhaps such things were important to fellow aristocrats. With his Scandinavian name she might well ask him the same question. If she was interested. Wiser not to go there.

'He made a fortune in the wool industry and helped out the king when he was short of cash,' she added. 'His reward was the title and the hand of Lady Elizabeth.'

'She didn't have a say in the matter?'

'A woman with land and a fortune had no say in who she married. She was property to be disposed of at the whim of her father, her brother or, in the absence of either, the king.' Aware that he had turned to look at her, she added, 'There was a bit of unpleasantness during the Commonwealth but Sir Ralph managed to keep his head and things returned to normal after the Restoration.'

'The new king also being short of money.'

'He owed a lot of people a lot of favours and those fancy wigs he wore cost a fortune.'

She might have got him with that one but just then, from the organ loft, the soft notes of Bach's 'Jesu, Joy of Man's Desiring' whispered across the church and he looked up, listened for a moment.

'Who is that playing?'

'Laura Chase. The vicar's wife. She plays for an hour every morning. She won't disturb us.'

'She's very good.'

He liked music? 'She trained at the Royal Academy. She was set for a career as a concert pianist, but then she met the Rev and gave it all up for love.'

Fredrik was staring at her. 'I imagine Hope will ask her to play at the wedding.'

'Combe St Philip has every talent on tap it would seem.'

Choosing not to rise to his unexpected irritation, Ally continued with the guided tour. 'Beneath the window is the tomb of Sir William de la Hase — '

'All very interesting no doubt,' Fredrik cut in, before she could enthuse on the beauty of the carved stone or point out the fact that the vaulted ceiling was very like the one in Bath Abbey. 'If I need a potted history of the church, I'll buy a guidebook.'

Ally, who had been determined to boost Hope's ancestry, her fitness to be a princess in the face of the disapproval of the royal family, had no choice but to leave it there.

'There's one in the folder I've prepared for you,' she said.

'Then let's not waste any more time on tombstones,' he said, not waiting for her to produce it from her bag, but heading up the aisle. 'What I need is a detailed layout of the church.' He took a small notebook and pen from his jacket pocket. 'How many doors are there?'

She'd blown up the layout of the church from the guidebook for him but suspected telling him that would simply irritate him further.

'Three. Apart from the great west door, there's a door in the tower, which is used by the bell ringers and there's an entrance to the vestry at the rear, which is used by the vicar and the choir.'

Without waiting to be asked she led the way to the tower.

Fredrik examined the heavy oak door, testing the ancient lock. 'They built to last in the fourteenth century,' he said, grudgingly, proving that he had been listening to her history lesson. 'This will have to be kept locked.'

Ally cleared her throat.

Fredrik turned to look at her. 'Is there a problem?'

'The bell ringers will need access,' she pointed out.

'They can come in through the church.'

'They can,' she agreed, 'but unless you expect them to stay in here throughout the entire wedding service, they will be tramping out again just as the bride is arriving and back in again at the end of the service.'

Fredrik gave her the kind of look that suggested bell ringers were his least favourite people in the entire world.

Or maybe it was her.

He was responsible for the safety of the royal family and faced with a situation that he could not control and unable to deploy a regiment of San Michele armed soldiers to guard them, she was the inevitable focus of his frustration.

Despite the unfairness of this, she felt an unexpected stab of sympathy. This must be his worst nightmare.

'Would you like to see the vestry?' she asked gently.

He glanced at her. 'Don't tell me,' he said. 'It's going to be the same story there.'

'The door has to be kept unlocked when there's a service.' She gave an apologetic little shrug. 'Fire regulations.' Wanting to help she added, 'The Chief Constable will be able to organize diplomatic protection for the royal family.'

'Armed?' he demanded.

'No!' Then, because of course DP

officers were armed, 'Well, yes, but Hope won't want guns at her wedding.'

'Then she should marry a country squire like her forebears,' he snapped.

'You think this is easy for her?' she snapped right back, well aware how Hope had struggled when she discovered that Jonas came with a ton of royal baggage. 'No one in their right mind would willingly put themselves through this.'

'So why is she?'

'Why did Laura Chase give up a career in music and marry the vicar? It's a mystery,' she said, answering her own question, 'but love falls where it will.'

'There is no obligation to pick it up,' he replied, his face like stone.

'You think she should have walked away? Is that what you would have done?'

'I can see why you wouldn't encourage her to do that,' he said, ignoring her question.

'Love that endures when everything is against it is a rare beast,' she said, choosing to ignore his dig at her.

'Something to be celebrated in Hope's wedding diary.'

A muscle was ticking in his jaw. What had she said?

'The diary that will make your fortune.'

Oh, that. 'Thank you for your confidence, sir,' she replied, injecting a fair bit of stone into her own voice, 'but every penny above the costs of printing and distribution of *Becoming a Princess* will go to Hope's charity.'

'Are you saying that you'll get nothing out of it?'

She hesitated.

It was going to be a heck of a lot of work but she would have done it for no other reason than Hope was her friend, for the sheer fun of being involved in a royal wedding. She couldn't deny, however, that she hoped to resurrect her career on the back of the diary.

'No,' she said. 'I'm not saying that.'

Maybe her frankness had finally silenced him, because there was no comeback.

'Shall we get on?' she suggested.

An hour later, having explored the crypt, climbed the tower, filled his notebook with sketches and measurements, and taken hundreds of photographs of the church and the ancient graveyard that surrounded it, they stood once more at the lychgate.

Fredrik looked up at the arch. 'This is going to be a problem.'

'Not at all,' Ally said. 'It will be covered with flowers and it will look fabulous.'

'I'm not talking about the aesthetics of the thing,' Fredrik said irritably. 'I'm concerned about security. I'd hoped to drive the royal party right up to the church door.' He bent to examine the footings more closely. 'I wonder how deep — ?'

'If you were about to suggest that it be removed, forget it,' Ally said quickly. 'Like the rest of the village it's Listed. With a capital L. That's a great big Do Not Touch notice, in case you were wondering. Besides, everyone will want to see the royal party arriving. What they're wearing. The villagers will line the way to watch Hope walk from the Hall on her brother's arm just as Kennard brides have done for centuries.'

'Walk?' He muttered an expletive. She raised her eyebrows and he apologized. 'I'm sorry.'

'I've heard worse and believe me, I do understand how difficult this must be for you.'

'I doubt it.'

Her phone rang at that moment and when Ally checked she saw that it was Flora Deare, the third in their all-for-one, one-for-all trio of friends. A supremely talented chef, she was in charge of catering the wedding and had moved into the Hall for the duration. She was also a fellow bridesmaid.

'I have to take this,' she said, but Fredrik was focused on the gate.

'Ally, where are you?' Flora asked.

'Outside the church.'

'What on earth are you doing there at

this time of the morning?' she asked, momentarily diverted. 'Oh, never mind. I need you!'

'Now? I'm a bit busy today.'

Flora, not in the mood to accept any excuses, said, 'Today isn't the problem. It's *tonight*. You've got to help me, Ally! We've got this Count from San Michele staying here.'

'So? You were expecting him weren't you?'

'How did you know? Sorry. I keep forgetting you're doing PR for Hope,' she said answering her own question. 'You know much more about what's going on than I do. Anyway, Hope asked if Max would put Fredrik up and as we're supposedly a couple, I'm staying there and playing hostess and . . . ' Ally snorted. 'Stop laughing! It's really awkward!'

'I can imagine,' she replied, doing her best to keep a straight face. Flora had confessed the pretend relationship over a glass or three of something chilled. None of it made sense to her, but presumably Flora knew what she was doing. 'Okay, Floradear,' she said, watching Fredrik as he paced the churchyard wall. 'What's the man done to get you in such a state?'

Stupid question. He didn't have to do anything but stand there looking dangerous.

'Nothing, He's just a bit intimidating. I mean, he's perfectly polite but he's so cool. He's got that whole sexy Special Forces thing going on, you know, all strong and silent, which is all very well until you're trying to have a conversation.' Cool and sexy . . . Not dangerous? Was she the only one who felt threatened? 'Max isn't Mr Chatty either,' Flora was saying, 'and the arrival of the stony-faced Count poking around every corner of the Hall looking for trouble has brought home the reality of what this wedding is going to involve. It was left to me to do all the talking last night, and I was exhausted by the time I went to bed.' She sounded seriously fed up.

'By yourself?' Ally asked, hoping to tease her out of it. 'Or did you have to be totally convincing. You know . . . with sound effects?'

'For goodness' sake, Ally! It's just a bit of play-acting,' Flora said, with rather more vehemence and a lot less humour than was normal.

'Sorry,' she said, but Ally's eyebrows had hit the roof. Had she inadvertently hit a raw spot? If she didn't know any better she'd think there really was something going on there . . . 'To be honest I'm having a bit of a weird one myself. Your Count caught me in full skivvy mode at the Three Bells this morning. Not exactly the impression I was hoping to make.'

'You've met him already? Well that's perfect! You can come to dinner tonight and use your famous charm to keep things ticking over while I'm in the kitchen doing my best to convince him that we're not going to put on a hog roast to feed our royal guests.'

A hog roast?

'I'm not sure he's impressed by my charm,' she said, her earlier Big Idea coalescing into something solid. 'He's pretty much accused me of encouraging Hope to marry her Prince in order to further my own ends.'

'Oh, for heaven's sake.'

'I know, but he's done a background check, Flora, and it was inevitable he'd think the worst.' She let it go, not wanting to depress Flora further. 'Don't worry. Once he's been softened up by your wonderful cooking it'll be a piece of cake to convince him that I'm not a wolf in rubber gloves and a pinny. I just hope Max is properly grateful for everything you're doing.'

'Not so you'd notice. I'd wittered on all evening and I'm sure Fredrik thought I was a complete airhead, but when I said that to Max, instead of saying of *course* I didn't come over as too silly for words and thanking me for doing all the work, all he said was that he wouldn't be surprised at all.'

'And he looks so sensible. Does he

know how lucky he is that you didn't crown him with a copper-bottomed saucepan?'

'There's still time. We've got to entertain the Count again tonight, so you've got to come and help, Ally. If nothing else, we can talk to each other.'

'Poor Floradear,' said Ally, amused. 'What's on the menu?'

'Chicken, quince and hazelnut ravioli to start, followed by roast haunch of venison with a potato and celeriac gratin and then lemon tart.' Flora rattled off the menu. 'What do you think?'

She thought that she wouldn't miss it for the world. She wanted to see Flora and Max together to find out what was really going on. What she said was, 'Make it those pear and chocolate puddings I like instead of lemon tart and you're on.'

'Chocolate will be too rich at the end of that meal.'

'Well, you *could* always chatter to Count Fredrik by yourself . . . '

Flora sighed. 'Chocolate and pear it is. Come about seven, okay? Wear something distracting.'

'I don't think Fredrik is a man to be diverted by a glimpse of gooseflesh.' Hasebury Hall was draughtier than a railway station. 'That ship sailed the minute he saw me in a headscarf and pink rubber gloves.' Not that anyone would have guessed from the fervour with which he'd kissed her. She could still feel —

'Rubbish,' Flora said. 'Do a Cinderella transformation and knock his socks off. I'll make sure Max piles the logs high in the grate.'

'Hope's the one with the Cinderella dress and glass slippers but I'll do my best,' she promised. 'It should be an interesting evening.'

Realizing that Fredrik had given up on the lychgate and was watching her through narrowed eyes, she said, 'Speaking of interesting, the man in question is eyeing the lychgate with the look of someone wondering where he can lay his hands on a chainsaw. I'd better go before he gets locked up.'

'Have you seen enough?' she asked, checking her watch as she rejoined Fredrik.

'Why? Are you in a hurry to be somewhere else?'

'The Old Forge,' she reminded him.

He frowned. 'That's all well and good for now,' he said, 'but as a bridesmaid you are part of the wedding party. You'll be expected to attend the reception and ball in San Michele next month when the palace make the official announcement.'

'I know. I have my invitation.'

'So? How will you manage?'

Good question. The truth was money was hideously tight and losing the best part of a week's wages was going to hurt but she wasn't going to tell him that.

'It's just a few days.'

Fortunately, much as she would love the excuse to sack her, Jennifer would keep her on just to be able to say that one of the royal bridesmaids was skivvying for her. And Penny, who ran the Old Forge, would certainly welcome the extra customers who would come in at lunchtime in the hope of being served by her.

It was going to be an interesting summer.

'If you've got a moment, I wanted to talk to you about the wedding diary.' His expression was not encouraging. 'The theme is 'Becoming a Princess'. We'll see Hope growing up, the story of how she and Jonas met and quotes from both families and photographs of the preparations for the wedding. I'm hoping that when I'm in San Michele I'll be able to talk to Jonas's family,' she said.

'You are very ambitious for a cleaning lady,' he said.

'Even cleaning ladies have dreams.' She had hoped he might return the favour and smooth the way for her but that was before she'd met him. 'I just need a sentence or two for the diary. All the proceeds will go to a charitable trust set up in Hope's name. I'm sure the royal family will want to support that?' When he didn't immediately answer, she added, 'Unless they want the entire world to know that they are not overjoyed at their youngest son's choice of bride?'

'Ambitious and sharp.'

She didn't think he was paying her a compliment.

'Since you'll want to come along and keep an eye on me, reassure yourself that I don't poke my nose behind the arras or sneak photographs of the royal knickknacks, I thought you might prefer to make the arrangements.'

'Knickknacks?'

Ally found herself wanting to reach out and use her thumb to wipe the frown from between his eyes. Wanting to see him smile.

Restraining herself, she said, 'I imagine in a palace they would be *objets d'art.*'

'I see. Perhaps it would just be easier

to confiscate your phone while you're in San Michele.'

'I'm pretty sure that would be an abuse of my human rights,' she said.

'Which right, specifically, would that be?'

'The right of every woman to have access to social media 24/7.' She tried a smile, hoping to tease him out of his grump. 'You'll just have to stay very close.'

'I intend to,' he replied, thoughtful rather than amused. 'You're taking on a great deal of work for someone who is not being paid.'

So much for charm, she thought, but she kept the smile pinned her lips as she shook her head. 'You know what they say about casting your bread upon the water,' she replied.

'That's what you're doing?' The question was apparently rhetorical since he did not wait for a reply but, pocketing his notebook, said, 'Thank you for your time, Ally, and the history lesson.'

'You're welcome,' she said, taking the

folder she'd prepared from her satchel and handing it to him. 'You'll find names and contact details of everyone you're likely to need in here. If there's anything else, email me.'

'Thank you. I'll see you next month in San Michele.'

'Yes,' she agreed, not bothering to tell him that he'd see her sooner than that. Her turn to surprise him. 'Are you going to Westonbury Court this afternoon?' she asked, to break that awkward silence when you've said goodbye but find yourself walking in the same direction. 'I'm not snooping, promise — ' she drew a cross over her heart with her finger ' — it's just that there are roadworks on the Ayesborough Road and although it's the long way around I think you'll find it quicker going through Upper Combe.'

4

Fredrik paused at the tall, wrought-iron gates of Hasebury Hall, watching as Ally walked away from him. Her long legs ate up the distance, her hair catching in the low shafts of sunlight as it swung around her shoulders.

She paused at the Market Cross, to respond to the query of a couple dressed for walking, looking at their map, smiling as she directed them on their way.

For a moment he was tempted to go after her, have a sandwich at the café where she worked the lunch shift, delaying his visit to Westonbury so that she could direct him through the narrow lanes.

Keeping her close, he told himself, was a duty.

A duty and a danger.

She'd made a living seducing the unwary with that smile and his default position was distrust.

He could still feel the heat of her lips as they'd responded to his, the jolt as his body had quickened, stirring from a long winter in response to something raw, something as elemental as lightning that had passed between them. The exhilaration of meeting a woman who could think so quickly on her feet when faced with an unexpected encounter.

She had anticipated his mistrust, too. Seemed to accept it as legitimate, putting his irritability down to that rather than the disturbing jolt to his libido. She had also managed, mostly, to hang on to her sense of humour in the face of some serious provocation, attempting to provoke a smile in return.

That he had found it so hard not to succumb warned him that she was very good at what she did, which made it all the more surprising that she hadn't been snapped up by another magazine.

All that would change the minute the news broke that she was at the heart of one of the biggest society weddings taking place this year.

She could sell news of the engagement now and pay off her debts with a substantial sum left over but she was cleverer than that.

As a bridesmaid she would be right at the centre of things and the wedding diary she was creating would give her access to the entire royal family. She would keep her secret until after the visit to San Michele. After that she would be able to deliver a scoop that would wipe out the opposition and set her up for life.

Casting her bread on the waters indeed . . .

Tucking the folder she'd given him under his arm, he took out his phone and made a call to the palace.

★　★　★

News of Fredrik's arrival had reached the Old Forge by the time she arrived for her shift.

'So? Who is the handsome stranger

who swept you off your feet this morning?' Penny asked, grinning, before she'd even got her coat off.

She rolled her eyes and grinned back. 'Good news travels fast.'

'I feel sorry for the guest speaker at the Women's Institute tonight. Forget jam and Jerusalem, you are going to be the sole topic of conversation. Your mother is going to be everyone's best friend.'

'Oh, joy.'

'So?'

'If you let me take a break in February,' she replied, 'I'll tell you everything when I get back.'

'Everything?'

'Everything that's fit to print.'

'Spoilsport. Dates?' she asked, turning to the calendar.

'The thirteenth to the seventeenth.'

'So you'll be away for Valentine's Day,' she said, pointedly.

'Really?' she said, innocently. 'I hadn't noticed.'

Fortunately they were too busy for Penny to dig further and by the time she got home her mother, who was president of the local WI, was too flustered by the imminent arrival of the County Organizer to ask more than if it was 'serious'.

Ally's reply, that it was 'too early to talk about', got one of her mother's looks, but for once she let it go at that.

★   ★   ★

The Hasebury Hall drawing room was empty, but the blaze in the hearth was inviting. Fredrik stood with his foot on the fender, the heat warming wounds that even though they were healed, still reacted badly to the cold.

He was looking into the flames, all attempts to concentrate on his schedule for the following day sabotaged by the memory of warm lips, a kiss, green-gold eyes that had stayed with him all day, when he heard the door open behind him.

He turned, a smile in place for Flora, who had tried desperately hard to make him feel welcome, and found himself face to face with the disturbing Miss Parker.

She'd disturbed him this morning when she was dressed down to clean the pub, her hair in a plait and without a scrap of make-up. Tonight, her mouth glistening a deep rose red in the fire-light, her hair pinned up in an apparently careless topknot, loose strands curling round a creamy skin left bare by a soft, jade green sweater that had slipped off one shoulder, she was off-the-scale trouble.

And he was right about the heels. She was wearing a pair of narrow black velvet pants and very high heels that gave the impression that her legs were endless.

'Ally . . . '

'Fredrik.'

'I did not realize that you would be joining us this evening.' She tilted her head to one side, a wry smile inviting him to try harder.

He was saved by Max.

'Ally!' he said. 'Flora told me you were coming. How lovely to see you.'

She flicked a glance at him as if to say that's how it's done before turning to Max.

'My treat, Sir Max. I never miss a chance to enjoy Flora's cooking.'

'Just Max, please. How are your parents?'

'Very well, thank you. My father sends his regards.'

He nodded. 'What can I offer you to drink?'

'A glass of wine?'

'I've opened the red we're having with dinner.'

'Perfect.'

Her smile filled the room and the empty shabbiness disappeared into the shadows as, settling herself into the corner of the sofa nearest to the fire, she crossed her long legs.

'Scotch, Fredrik?'

It took a moment for Max's offer to infiltrate. 'Oh, yes. Thank you.'

'Did you have a productive afternoon?' Ally asked when they were alone.

'Useful.' Her sweater slipped a little

lower, the exposed strap of her underwear a blatant invitation to slip a finger beneath it, leaving the silky skin of her shoulder at the mercy of his mouth . . . He swallowed, cleared his throat. 'Thank you for the comprehensive folder you prepared. It's been very . . . '

She arched a brow. 'Useful?'

'Yes.' He made an effort to focus. 'I spoke to Princess Anna this afternoon. She informs me that you will not be bringing a partner to San Michele.' It had suited his plan to keep her close while she was in San Michele, but now he wasn't so sure. 'I would have thought there'd be a queue to join you.'

'I'm sure you meant that as a compliment, Fredrik, and no doubt I could have found someone.' Her shoulder moved in the smallest of shrugs, the implication being that she could have had her pick of men to squire her. 'I'm sure my ex-boss would have leapt at the chance.' She smiled to show that was teasing. 'Somehow I don't think he'd have been welcome.' She put her head to one side drawing attention to long jade earrings that exactly matched her sweater. 'Do I get a black mark from Princess Anna for messing up her seating plan for the banquet?'

'On the contrary — she was relieved. She needed a spare woman to partner someone at the reception and ball.'

'Oh? Is this where I get my prince?' she asked. 'I believe Prince Nico is unattached at the moment.'

'I'm sorry to disappoint you but Princess Anna has other plans for him. You'll have to make do with me.'

'Well that's perfect. You'll be able to keep me under close surveillance.' She gave him a cool look from beneath ridiculously long lashes. Was she flirting with him? Did she think she could seduce him into forgetting his doubts about her? 'I hope you can dance . . . '

The words died on her lips and a flush darkened her cheekbones. She'd obviously read about his close encounter with the grim reaper and was dearly wishing the words safely back behind her teeth. Until now she'd had him on the back foot but her embarrassment — a first hint of fallibility — gave him the advantage for once.

'Save the slow dances for me and I'll probably manage,' he said, intending to press it home, but succeeding only in imagining what it would be like to hold her close. In those high heels she had been looking him straight in the eye. A perfect fit . . .

'Sorry to be so long. Flora needed a hand . . . ' The reappearance of Max, bearing drinks, gave them both a moment to recover. 'You looked around the church this morning, I understand,' he said, handing a glass of red wine to Ally and then passing him his Scotch. 'Is it going to be big enough?'

'That depends. It's surprisingly large for such a small place but if Hope plans to invite the entire village it's going to be a bit of a squeeze.'

'Combe St Philip was an important centre of the wool trade in the Middle

Ages,' Ally explained. She took a sip from the glass of wine that Max had handed her, licking a drop from her lips. 'Rich merchants bought their way into heaven by building churches. The bigger, the more ornate . . . ' Her voice trailed away as she realized that he was watching her and she turned to Max. 'Have you talked to the vicar, yet? We need to make sure the church remains free for the wedding.'

'I thought I should leave it until after the announcement.'

'Leave what?' Flora asked, backing into the room, both hands full with trays of canapes.

He hated fussy bits of food but, grateful for any distraction, he crossed to hold the door for her. 'Thank you, Fredrik.'

'Max needs to ask the vicar to save the day before someone else grabs the church for a concert or flower festival,' Ally said. 'You know how it gets booked up in the summer. Actually, he should take it off the books straight after

Sunday evensong and ask The Friends of St Philip to give it a thorough clean on the Monday.'

'But he'll want to know why,' Max protested.

'Just be your usual vague self, darling,' Flora said. 'Tell him you'll give him the details in a week or two. Fredrik, will you give me your opinion on these? Do you think any of these would be suitable to serve at the reception?'

'They are gorgeous, Flora,' Ally said, when he'd mumbled something about asking Hope and Jonas. She popped something small and pink into her mouth, then, having regained her composure, she patted the seat beside her. 'I'm getting a crick in my neck looking up at you all. Come and sit down, Fredrik, and tell us what's going to happen when we get to San Michele.'

The sofas, he had already discovered, were old and saggy. He sat at the far end so that they wouldn't be thrown together and gave them the news that they would be flying by private jet to San Michele, along with the bare bones of their itinerary while they were there.

Ally and Flora wanted all the details, fizzing with excitement at the prospect of a reception, banquet and ball to celebrate the engagement. They talked dresses over dinner and wanted to know if they would get a chance to see any of the country. Max, whose life was being disrupted at great personal expense to give his sister the wedding she wanted, seemed distracted until Ally announced that she'd had a great idea.

'Hope wants a village wedding. Obviously you're not going to invite the entire village. We can't fit everyone in the church and the reception is very much for family and close friends.' She took a breath. 'I think the answer to getting everyone involved is to throw a wedding party on the green.'

'A party?' Max asked, startled out of his thoughts.

'A celebration they can all be part of,' Ally explained. 'And a thank you for all the inevitable disruption the wedding will cause.'

Max might have groaned but Flora said, 'What exactly were you thinking, Ally?'

'A marquee, food, a bouncy castle for the kids, maybe one of those lovely carousels, some basic sideshows and music of some sort. For dancing.'

'Dancing on the green?'

'We can put down a wooden floor.'

Max rolled his eyes but Flora, ever practical, said, 'Who is going to do the catering?'

'Not you, Floradear. You have enough on your plate already.'

A little chocolate from the pudding was smeared on her upper lip and as she licked it away Fredrik missed Flora's response.

'I've given it some thought and there are three options. We could run it like a traditional street party where everyone contributes something. Didn't the WI coordinate the party for the Diamond Jubilee?' she asked Max.

'It rained,' he replied, gloomily.

'It's not going to rain on Hope's wedding,' Ally said patiently. 'I won't allow it.'

She caught his eye and Fredrik found himself fighting a smile. It wasn't funny. She had the quiet persistence of a mole. You'd only know you had a problem when a pile of trouble was tossed up in the middle of all your neatly laid plans.

'Option two,' she continued, 'is to have the Three Bells and the Old Forge provide a hot and cold buffet. That would have the advantage of keeping Jennifer Harmon sweet.'

Flora pulled a face. 'There isn't enough sugar in the world to sweeten that woman. Fortunately she employs good people in the kitchen. What's option three?'

'We could ask Jeff Thomas to do one of his hog roasts.' Getting no response to that she said, 'There is a fourth option.'

'We forget it,' Max suggested, under his breath.

Ally, choosing not to hear that, said, 'I think we should do a combination of all three and keep everyone happy.'

'Cakes from the WI, main food catered, a hog roast for the evening?' Flora said. 'That sounds perfect. What does Hope think?'

'I wanted to run it past you before I suggested it.' She looked across at him. 'Fredrik? Will it be a problem for you?'

He shrugged. 'It has the advantage of keeping everyone in the same place and fully occupied.'

'Max?'

'Who is going to organize all this?'

'I will,' Ally said.

He sighed, nodded. 'Hope will love it.'

'Flora?'

'Max is right. Hope will adore it and it will bring the whole village together which is exactly what she wants.'

'And if it does rain?' Fredrik could not resist teasing her. 'This is England.'

'There will be cloudless blue skies over Combe St Philip for the entire week,' she assured him. 'But, in the unlikely event that a shower has the bad manners to lose its way, we will move the dance to the village hall.'

'And the hog roast?'

'Jeff Thomas has been doing them for years. He's prepared for all eventualities but he is in demand so we'll have to book him straight away. I can talk to him but he'll want a deposit.'

Max nodded. 'Tell me what you need and I'll sort it.'

When Ally and Flora left to make coffee Max shook his head. 'That woman is like her mother. Unstoppable.'

He'd met her mother and survived to tell the tale. Ally was something else.

'She and Hope are close?' he asked.

'They bonded at infant school but didn't see much of each other when Hope went away to boarding school. When the old man made an idiot of himself there was no money for that so she had to come home and go to the local high school. Posh kid brought down to earth,' he said. 'As you can imagine, she had a pretty rough time of it.' He shook his head, staring into his glass. 'I was trying to hang on to the estate, my marriage was falling apart and I was worried to death about the children. Hope, I'm ashamed to say, was left to get on with it. It was Ally who was there for her, at school and in the village.'

'But Flora is older.'

'I suppose so.' It didn't seem to have occurred to him that it was unusual. 'I've no idea how the three of them became so close, but she's been like a big sister to Hope. The really good kind.' He looked up. 'Do you have family, Fredrik?'

'Too many,' he said, bitterly. Realizing from Max's raised eyebrows that he'd betrayed feelings that he normally kept well hidden, he forced a smile. 'I have a younger brother and sister and my mother has two more children with her second husband.' Seeing the question, he said, 'My father died when I was eleven.'

'I'm sorry.'

He shrugged, looked up as the women rejoined them, laughing, obviously close. He was the outsider as Ally and Flora, with the occasional suggestion from Max, discussed the arrangements for the village green party. It was Ally who made an effort to include him, taking the time to tell him who they were talking about, sharing the outrageous foibles of people they'd known all their lives.

Finally, though, she said, 'Floradear, that was the most wonderful meal but Jennifer wants me in an hour earlier tomorrow so I'm going to have break up the party or I'll sleep through the alarm.'

'Really? Surely they're not that busy at this time of year?'

Ally shook her head, raised an eyebrow. 'I'll give you a call tomorrow.'

They exchanged a look. Clearly there was something she didn't want to say in front of Max. Or was it him?

'I was thinking, if you're organizing all this as well as Hope's wedding diary you're going to need somewhere to work. We can find her a room here, can't we, Max?'

Max agreed that there was no shortage of rooms.

'That would be great. I'm trying to keep everything under wraps but Mum will *clean*.'

'Come over after you've finished tomorrow,' Flora suggested. 'About ten? That's if Fredrik doesn't need you?'

He shook his head. 'I'm seeing the Chief Constable first thing and then going straight on to the airport. Thank you again for your hospitality. The wedding reception is in good hands,' he added.

Flora blushed. 'Thank you. There's always a bed here if you need to come back.' Then, turning to Max: 'Will you walk Ally home, darling?'

Ally opened her mouth, clearly about to object, but Flora gave her a fierce look and Fredrik heard himself saying, 'I could do with some fresh air. I'll see Ally safely home.'

She looked straight at him and for a

moment he thought she was going to tell him there was no need, that she could manage, and he didn't know whether he wanted her to wave off his company or smile and say, 'Thank you.' Ally Parker sparked off a whole load of danger signals. That sideways look she'd been giving him all evening, an unreadable smile, left him feeling like a cat whose fur had been rubbed up the wrong way.

Before she could do or say anything, Flora accepted on her behalf.

Ally and Flora hugged, Max kissed her cheek and then they were in the ancient panelled hall and he was helping her into a long black coat that was a million miles away from the padded jacket she'd worn that morning. No doubt her job at the gossip magazine had required a quality wardrobe and the kind of grooming that wouldn't make her look out of place amongst the celebrities she interviewed.

'How are you going to manage in those heels?' he asked, as she draped a long, brightly coloured scarf around her neck.

'I have years of practice,' she said, producing a pair of fine gloves and a small torch from her coat pocket. 'Shall we go?'

5

The driveway was pitch-dark once they left the area close to the Hall. There was no moon but in the clear frosty night the payoff was a sky filled with stars.

Ally stopped to look up. 'What an amazing sight. You never see this in London.'

'Nor in Liburno, but up in the mountains the stars are so thick and close that it feels as if you could reach up and scoop a handful.'

How long had it been?

'You must miss it. Climbing?' she prompted, distracting him.

Miss it?

It was like the phantom pain of a missing limb . . .

'I'm too busy to waste time worrying about what I can't do.' He took the torch from her, using it to light the uneven path ahead of them. 'I can see why Flora asked Max to see you home.'

She didn't move for a moment and then, accepting that he wasn't going to talk about climbing, said, 'I could have managed but you were coming out for a breath of fresh air and Floradear worries about me walking home alone in the dark.'

'Why?'

'She thinks I'll break my neck in these shoes.'

The look that had passed between them suggested something more but he let it go. 'Why do you call her Floradear?'

'It's her name. Flora Deare. Hope ran it together years ago and it stuck because that's exactly what she is. Flora-dear.'

'Max said she was like a big sister to both you and Hope. That you were both kind when he wasn't there for her.'

'Poor man. His wife was no support when his life fell apart. She didn't stick around while he was forced to sell most of his land, the furniture, silver, paintings collected over centuries, just to hang on to the Hall. His children were his first concern and I suppose he thought Hope was old enough to take care of herself.'

'He sees them? His children?'

'Oh, yes. His wife remarried surprisingly quickly but they all get on pretty well. His little girl is going to be one of Hope's bridesmaids. His son, unsurprisingly, refused point-blank to be a page. They're going to San Michele with Max and Flora.'

'Yes, I know.'

'Of course you do.' Her heard the amusement in her voice. 'You know everything.'

'I'm glad you think so.'

She glanced sideways at him. 'I'll tell you anything you want to know, Fredrik.'

'Will you?' He had a dozen questions burning his tongue but none of them had anything to do with the wedding. 'Tell me why Max is putting himself through this when he obviously hates every minute of it.'

'Hope's father was undoubtedly a

fool, but she was only fourteen when he died in prison. No one had a good word to say for him and I'm not sure that anyone really understood how hard it hit her. He was still her dad and she loved him.'

'Of course she did.' The words came through a throat thick with memory.

'Max knows he let her down. Giving his sister her perfect wedding is his chance to make up for not being there when she needed him.'

They had reached the gate and he opened the small personnel gate for her but, as she stepped through, she stumbled on those ridiculous heels and he made a grab for her arm. There was a small, strangled sound — the kind a person makes when their throat is closed with fear, and Ally swung round to face him, eyes wide, arms up in a defensive gesture.

'Ally . . . '

She quickly lowered her hands. 'Sorry.' She shook her head. 'Sorry . . . ' she repeated, then turned and walked quickly away, the sound of her heels echoing off the terraced houses that lined the narrow street.

The village was not quite as dark as the Hall driveway. Some of the cottages had lamps over the doors and there was light from a few windows but there were no street lamps. The lane was full of ink-black shadows. He lost sight of her once and hurried to catch up.

'What happened?' he asked, as he caught up, fell in beside her. 'What did I do?'

'It's nothing. Stupid. An old story.' But important, obviously. 'It's nothing,' she repeated.

'That was a classic PTSD response,' he said. She glanced at him. 'With me it's paper ripping.'

'Paper?'

'It's exactly the sound of an incoming shell,' he said. 'The first few times I heard it I threw myself under the nearest desk. Not a great image when you're head of security.' He wasn't going to tell her about the nights he'd woken up screaming . . . 'Jonas persuaded me to talk to someone. Bottling it up doesn't help.'

'Flora and Hope know,' she said.

Of course they did. They had protected her, kept her secret. 'The fear is still there, Ally. You need to talk to someone who isn't emotionally involved.'

'You?'

'Lack of emotional involvement is my default setting and discretion goes with the job.' He gave her a moment, then said, 'You did say that you would tell me anything I asked.'

Ally shivered as a tawny owl hooted its familiar call from a tall perch in the churchyard before drifting on silent wings across the lane in front of them and into the grounds of the Hall.

It was true. She'd said that because she wanted him to trust her. But telling him about her darkest moment was more about whether she trusted him.

'You're cold,' he said, stopping to take off his scarf, holding it so that she could see what he was doing before wrapping it gently around her neck, taking care not to make any sudden movements. His thoughtfulness, his understanding of her nervousness should have made her feel cared for, but it just made her feel pathetic.

That wasn't her. She'd walked through the night-time streets of London without a qualm. It was only here, in the village, that she feared the shadows.

As if she'd never grown past that moment.

Maybe she hadn't.

Hope and Flora were protective, aware that it was as real to her as if it had happened yesterday. Perhaps he was right that she needed to talk about it and maybe, if she told Fredrik what had happened, he'd understand why she would never betray Hope.

There was a stone bench outside the churchyard. She crossed to it, sat down, arms wrapped tightly around her. He joined her, not too close, careful not to be threatening. Not nearly close enough . . .

'I was sixteen,' she began, 'and thought I knew everything.'

'We've all been there. It's called growing up.' She looked at him, wondering what he'd done when he was sixteen, hoping that he'd share some scrape. 'Another time,' he said. 'This is your story.'

'Yes.' Her throat was thick with tension and she took a minute to breathe, force herself to relax. 'It was a Saturday. I told my parents that I was going to spend the night with a friend but I was actually going to a club in Ayesborough with a girl from school.' She pulled a face. 'Lily Peters was the kind of girl my mother would have thought 'unsuitable'.'

'Was she?'

'Oh, yes.' It was probably the first time she'd ever admitted her mother had been right about anything and oddly, it made her feel better. 'She was the queen of one of those cliques at school that everyone wanted to part of. They wore too much make-up, skirts up to their backsides and were always surrounded by boys.'

'You're telling me that the boys weren't lining up to date you?' he asked. He sounded genuinely surprised.

'I was a TPV.' She pulled a face. 'A teacher's pet virgin.'

He made a sound that was somewhere between a cough and a splutter. 'Where was Hope?' he managed.

'Hope?'

'You were friends. Wasn't she in on this?'

'Oh, no, she had a job working in the kitchen at the Three Bells on Saturday nights. I wanted to work there but my mother refused point-blank. Max would probably have done the same but he had other things on his mind and Hope needed the money.' She glanced at him. 'I finally got what I wanted. Ironic or what?'

'Deeply. What happened, Ally?'

She shrugged. 'Lily suddenly became friendly, asked me if I wanted to join them in Ayesborough on Saturday night.'

'Why did you go?'

'I thought that if I was one of them,

people would stop giving Hope a hard time. Teenage girls can be vile.' She looked up at the stars. There had been none that night. It had been overcast, dark as pitch. 'She lived a couple of miles away in Upper Combe but she told me if I waited in the Three Bells car park they'd pick me up at nine o'clock. I was already nervous, wishing I was safely home but even more afraid of looking a fool, knowing that if I copped out it would be ten times worse at school.'

As if he knew what that had felt like, Fredrik held out a hand and gratefully, she took it, held it.

'I hid out of sight in the darkest corner of the car park for what seemed like hours. I'd just about given up, relieved that I could go home, when someone reached out and grabbed my shoulder. My nerves were in shreds by then and I let out an almighty scream. The next thing I knew there was a hand over my mouth, I was pinned to the wall, there was this voice in my ear

100

growling at me to be quiet and there was a hand . . . '

She swallowed. Every sound, every touch, the way her heart had jumped as he'd grabbed her was imprinted on her memory, the raw terror as vivid now as it had been in the dark of the car park.

'I bit him and kicked out, trying to bring my heel down his shin. He backed off to avoid me but lost his balance, falling against one of the bins, taking me down with him.'

Fredrik's hand tightened around hers as if he could give her his strength. He had been through far worse than her and survived.

She had survived.

'How did you escape?'

'How do you know I did?'

'Because if he'd assaulted you there would have been records. They would have shown up when I ran my security check.'

'Only if I reported it.'

'Why wouldn't you?'

She looked at him. 'Because it would

have got my parents involved; everyone would have known what happened. Can you imagine what that would have been like? At school, in the village?'

The gossip, the smirks, the innuendo.

'We'll never know what he might have done because Flora and Hope came charging out of the pub kitchen like the seventh cavalry.'

'Flora?'

'She was working as assistant chef at the Three Bells back then. She thought it was a fox at the bins but when she realized what was happening she laid about him with the stainless steel ladle she was holding with Hope right behind her with a saucepan.'

'Were you hurt?'

'No. Scared witless, shaking like a jelly, but not hurt. He was just a stupid boy, Fredrik. It was his sister I was supposed to be meeting. He knew she wasn't coming . . . '

A teenage boy whose hormones were out of control.

'Flora took me into the kitchen, gave

me a cup of sweet tea and, when I'd stopped shaking, something to eat. When they finished work Flora walked us both back to the Hall and I spent the night with Hope.'

'What about the boy? Did they just let him go?'

'They debagged him, took photos with their phones and warned him they would pin them to the village hall notice-board if he said one word about what had happened. If he ever so much as looked at a girl the wrong way. Then they sent him home with his backside freezing and crying like a baby.'

'He knew you'd be alone, Ally. He grabbed you out of the dark and you shivered this morning when I helped you on with your coat. I thought you were cold, but I'd put my hand on your shoulder . . . '

'I was a bit unnerved by your unexpected arrival,' she admitted. By a kiss that had come out of the blue and for which she was unprepared. It had slipped past an emotional guard of which, until that moment, she had been scarcely aware.

'I'm sorry, Ally. I hope you know that I would never hurt you.' He shook his head. 'No. Of course you don't know that. How would you?'

She squeezed his hand hoping to reassure him. 'I . . . We were both taken by surprise this morning.'

'Yes . . . ' He stood up, helped her to her feet and then, when she was standing beside him, he tucked her hand beneath his arm and they walked slowly up the hill to her parents' cottage.

'I sometimes wonder how he explained his missing trousers,' she said after a while.

'Not your worry.'

'No.' She looked sideways at him. 'Thank you.'

'For what?'

'Talking it through with someone neutral, someone who wasn't angry at what happened, has helped.' He glanced at her. 'It was the trousers. Thinking about him walking home, ducking into a hedge whenever a car came by, praying that no one would see him,' she said. 'It made me realize that he probably has night-mares about it, too.'

'The difference being that in his case he deserves them. We all have to take responsibility for what we do.'

'Yes.' She hesitated, then said, 'If you ever want someone to talk to, Fredrik, I'm a good listener, too and I have more secrets in my head than you can ever know.' When he didn't reply — why would he spill his terrors to a woman who had written for a gossip rag? — she said, 'You'd better take the torch.'

'You'll need it tomorrow if you're going to work before dark. I'll use the one on my phone.'

She took her key from her pocket, slid it into the lock then turned back to him. 'You're leaving tomorrow?'

'After I've talked to the Chief Constable.'

'My email address and phone number are in the file I gave you. If you need anything . . . information . . . ' She stopped. Call me, sounded needy.

'I'll be in touch,' he said. 'And I'll see you in San Michele three weeks from now.'

'I'll hold you to that dance,' she said. 'Travel safely, Fredrik.'

He took the hand she offered, held it. 'You do realize that if anyone sees us shaking hands it's going to blow the 'us' scandal right out of the water?'

She swallowed. 'Are you suggesting that we should go for another kiss? Just to preserve the fantasy?'

'In security, when you're playing a role, you have to stay in character and it was you who told me that in a village everyone knows your business.'

She swallowed, not able to remember the last time she had so longed for someone to kiss her. 'It would be fatal to destroy the legend,' she agreed.

'Goodnight, Ally.' There was a touch of warmth as he brushed his lips to her cheek and then as he raised her hand to his lips, the church clock began to chime the hour.

Before she could think of anything to say, he'd reached up, turned the key in the lock and pushed the door open, waiting until she had stepped inside before he turned and walked away into the darkness.

⋆　⋆　⋆

'Thanks,' Ally said as Flora handed her a mug of coffee, but she shook her head at the temptation of cake. 'Better not if I'm going to fit into my dress.'

Flora joined her at the window where she was enjoying the drifts of snow-drops whitening the grass beneath the yellow fuzz of the witch hazel in the Hasebury Hall garden.

'I can't believe that tomorrow we'll be guests of the San Michele royal family. Staying in a palace,' she said. 'What did you tell your mum and dad?'

Ally turned from the window. 'The truth. That Hope has fixed me up with a PR gig.'

'You got away with that?'

'She didn't press for details but that's because she thinks that I'm actually off for a few days of hot sex with the mysterious Fredrik.' A thought that sent a tingle of anticipation whispering through her veins. 'The fact that she offered to iron some stuff for me suggests she's hoping for something more permanent.'

Flora grinned. 'Wait until she finds out he's a count.'

The three weeks since Fredrik's visit had flown. Max had found her a large room upstairs at the back of the house. It must once have been a sitting room and was furnished with a sofa, an armchair and not much else. He'd moved in a table that she was using as a desk, had found her a long trestle table that was now piled up with media packs and an old fold-out screen that she'd used for her layout ideas for the diary.

She'd scanned the mock-ups and loaded them onto her tablet to show Hope when they were in San Michele.

She just had to decide which she liked best and she'd be ready to go.

She had a huge planner across one wall with everything she had to do marked off. Jeff Thomas had been booked — he hadn't cared about the occasion, just about his deposit. Tick. The vicar had booked the church under the impression that there was going to be some kind of craft exhibition that week. Max could do a very good 'vague'.

'Are you all ready, Floradear?' Ally asked. 'I can't wait to see you in the dress you bought for the ball. Max's eyes will be out on stalks.'

Colour flashed across Flora's cheeks. 'I'm dreading wearing those heels. I don't know how you do it.'

'Just stand up straight and think of England.'

She pulled a face. 'I'll probably fall into someone's lap. How are you getting to the airport? I wish we could have offered you a lift but you do not ever want to ride in the back with the children. Holly is a sweetheart, but Ben bounces. He couldn't sit still for five seconds.'

'Actually . . . ' Ally cleared her throat and Flora looked up. 'Fredrik has arranged for a car to pick me up.'

'Fredrik?' She raised an eyebrow.

'Don't look at me like that,' she said, aware that it was her turn to blush. 'Neither of us has a partner so the Crown Princess has put us together. Protocol, appearances . . . ' She rolled her eyes. 'It seems that a woman can't go into dinner or to a ball without a man on her arm. We're just like you and Max.' Although, on reflection, Flora and Max seemed rather closer than convenient partners these days so that might not be the best comparison. 'I guess, as my official 'date' he's taking his role seriously,' she rushed on.

'More likely her Serene Highness wants to keep you safely out of the reach of Prince Nico. She won't want any more village maidens running off with the San Michele princes.'

'I've met Nico.'

'No! What's he like?'

'Absolutely gorgeous. Film star looks, great sense of humour . . . '

'That sounds promising.'

'He's also a playboy who can't see a pretty woman without falling in love. Fun, but not to be taken seriously.'

'You could do with some fun. I can't see Fredrik providing that.' When she didn't immediately agree, Flora looked at her thoughtfully. 'Unless something happened on that long walk home in the dark that you're not telling me about?'

'He was a perfect gentleman.'

'Really? How disappointing,' she said and they both burst out laughing.

6

Ally had flown in private jets before, but that had been work. She'd been the journalist writing up a WAG's hen trip to a spa resort in the Far East, or covering a spread about some fabulous celebrity home in the Caribbean. An observer, an outsider who, once the photo shoot was done, flew home cattle class.

This trip was a world away from that.

She would be staying at the palace in San Michele's capital, Liburno. A guest of the royal family and, as if to emphasize that difference, Hope and Jonas were waiting on the tarmac as the plane taxied to a halt a little distance from the terminal building.

She looked around, then forgot her disappointment that Fredrik wasn't there, as Hope hugged her, Jonas kissed her cheek. Flora, Max and the children were loaded into one limousine and within minutes she was being driven through the quaint, colourful streets of Liburno with Hope and her prince.

People turned as they saw the flag fluttering above the windscreen, waved. She and Hope exchanged a glance as Jonas waved back, then burst into giggles.

'Shouldn't you be doing that?' she asked Hope, but she shook her head.

'Not until after the announcement. Not then if I can help it.'

'They'll think you're stuck-up. You have to be a people's princess these days,' she said, meaning it as a joke, but Hope looked away, the moment of silliness over. Without the smile the strain of what must be a nerve-racking few days clearly showed. Ally grasped her hand, squeezed it and got a grateful smile in return.

'I've got some mock-ups of the diary for you to look at,' Ally said. 'And I've made a start with photographs. When you've got a moment.'

'It's a bit late today. You'll need time to settle in and get ready for the reception. Tomorrow morning?'

'Perfect.' She looked up as they approached the castle and although she'd seen photographs online she still gasped. 'It's amazing.'

'The State Rooms are impressive,' Jonas said, 'and the guest suites. They're maintained by the Government. Once you get further back to the offices and the family apartments there's rather more functionality and comfort than glamour.'

'I imagine all palaces are the same,' Ally said. 'I did a tour of Buckingham Palace last year and those State Rooms aren't exactly built for comfort. I mean you couldn't put your feet up and relax.'

Jonas was grinning as he climbed from the car and offered a hand to both her and Hope. That was the thing about princes: they had such lovely manners.

The car with Flora, Max and the children drew up behind them and as

Jonas went back to welcome them to the palace, Hope hugged Ally again.

'I'm so glad you're here,' she said, a touch of desperation in her voice.

'Hope? Is everything okay?'

'What? Oh, absolutely. Fine,' she said, but her smile seemed forced. 'It's all just a bit . . . you know.'

Actually she did. She'd been in the background at numerous high-profile weddings and seen the tension rise to cracking point. A royal wedding had to be that magnified a dozen times over.

'Breathing helps,' she said. 'And gin. Lots of gin.'

Hope laughed, shook her head and, leaving them in the hands of a footman, gathered up Holly and Ben and announced that she was taking them to meet Jonas's nephews and niece. 'I'll see you all later.'

Ally, more concerned than her flippant advice suggested, decided to talk to Flora and see if the royal itinerary would allow time for the three of them to get together.

Then, as the footman opened the door to her room fit for a prince she momentarily forgot Hope as she let out a very uncool, 'Wow.'

There was a magnificent marble fireplace that, before the installation of central heating, would have blazed with logs piled up to warm the royal tootsies.

The ceiling was massively high, as were windows — swagged with a rich ruby red velvet — that looked out over the palace gardens to the ancient town and harbour. The furniture gleamed with the patina of centuries of use, the rugs were Persian and there was a four-poster bed that she was going to need a stepladder to climb into.

A knock distracted her and her heart lifted a beat. 'Come in.'

It was not Fredrik, but a footman with her luggage. 'Do you require help unpacking, ma'am?' he asked.

'I can manage, thank you,' she said.

'Of course. If you need anything just ring the bell.'

He indicated a damask bell pull with

a large gold tassel that hung beside the fireplace and then, with the merest suggestion of a bow, left her to explore.

On a table near the window there was a tray with a bowl of fruit, a bottle of water, glasses. And a square, cream envelope. Written across the front in a clear, bold hand was '*Miss Alice Parker*'.

Heart seriously pounding now she picked it up, turned it over. It bore a coat of arms on the flap — not the Reval family coat of arms — with a Latin motto beneath it. *Ex fortitudine patria* . . .

She opened it and slid out a card that read simply, 'A footman will collect you at 1815 hrs and escort you to the main hall. Drinks in the Green Drawing Room at 1830 hrs precisely. Fredrik.'

A footman? 1815 hrs?

Could it be any colder?

She swallowed down her disappointment.

They'd exchanged a few emails, all very businesslike and impersonal, but he'd kissed her hand and she'd expected . . . What? That he'd be so impatient to see her he'd be waiting at the airport?

This was Fredrik Jensson. He didn't do excited and clearly she'd misread the personal.

He'd listened as she'd spilled out her night of shame but no doubt that was all part of the security chief's job. Getting close to those who might be a problem, discovering all their little weaknesses. And she'd made it so easy for him.

She closed the hand he'd kissed, tightening it into a fist. Was that part of the job, too? Like the car?

He hadn't asked her how she was getting to the airport, he'd simply sent details of the booking he'd made for a car to pick her up. Not the local taxi, but a limousine driven by a uniformed chauffeur. She would have thought it part of the travel arrangements organized by Jonas, but Max, Flora and the children had gone to the airport in Max's Range Rover.

She'd thought, hoped, that it had

been a personal kindness. Clearly not. He was her official 'date' for the weekend — by royal appointment.

There was another knock and despite the card in her hand her heart lifted as she turned and the door opened.

It was a maid with a tray. 'Miss Kennard thought you would like tea, ma'am,' the young woman said, setting down the tray in front of her. 'Is there anything else you need? Would you like me to press the dress you'll be wearing this evening?'

She was an experienced packer. Her dress would emerge from the layers of tissue with scarcely a crease but the girl was so eager to do something that she found a smile from somewhere. 'That would be very kind. What's your name?'

'Luisa, ma'am.'

'Thank you for the tea, Luisa. Please don't call me ma'am. I'm not the queen. I'm Ally. Now, shall we see what the damage is?'

She opened her case, found the dress she'd chosen for the evening. Her working wardrobe was largely of the LBD variety, nothing cut too low — she took great care not to appear a threat to the celebrities she interviewed — but she had a few choice pieces picked up in a vintage store run by a woman who owed her many favours. She'd chosen a wraparound knee-length dress from the 50s in teal crepe. The V-neck plunged, but discreetly and the dress hugged her figure without looking vulgar. It emerged from her case with scarcely a wrinkle, nothing that an hour on a hanger wouldn't have sorted, but Luisa tutted and bore it away, promising to return it in plenty of time for the reception.

Ally stood at the window, sipping her tea, taking in the old town that clustered around the palace and flowed down the hill towards the harbour. She was eager to get out and explore, take some photographs.

There were a couple of hours before she had to get ready and no one had offered her better entertainment so, hooking her bag over her shoulder, she retraced her steps through the palace, only taking the wrong turn once.

As she passed through the vast arched gateway a couple of soldiers snapped to attention. She tried to look as if this happened to her all the time and kept going.

★   ★   ★

'I'm sorry to bother you, sir ... ' Fredrik, who'd been reading the same paragraph of a report for the last ten minutes and still hadn't a clue what it said, looked up, relieved to be interrupted. 'I thought you'd want to know that one of the English visitors has just left the palace.'

'Which one?' As if he need ask.

'Miss Parker, sir. Shall I send someone after her? In case she gets lost,' he added, but Fredrik was already on his feet.

'I'll go.' If the duty officer was surprised, he knew better than to show it. 'She'll be nervous if she's approached by someone she does not know.'

'Of course, sir.'

He'd been doing his best not to think about her but the kiss they'd shared was imprinted on his brain. He caught himself smiling at her attempts to tease him out of his bad mood, her flirtatiousness over dinner at the Hall, their walk back to the village in the dark. Still found himself tensing as he remembered how she'd opened up to him and shared her worst moment.

She had slipped beneath his defences, got into his head, arousing him for the first time since he'd forced Eloise to walk away.

He'd managed to keep their communications impersonal, strictly business, resisting the temptation to call her on some pretext and build on the connection they'd made.

His determination to keep her at a distance had taken a serious hit when he'd seen her arrive on the CCTV cameras covering the main entrance of the palace. She'd stopped for a moment, looked around, then up at the CCTV camera and smiled as if she knew he was there, watching. Then Hope had hugged her and she'd turned away.

He caught sight of her soon enough.

She had been taking her time, strolling down through the old town, taking photographs — not on her phone like most tourists, but with a high-end compact SLR camera.

She'd discarded the jacket of the grey pinstripe trouser suit she'd been wearing when she arrived, her deep pink shirt making her easy to spot as people began to come back onto the streets after the long break for lunch.

Her hair was loose, the sun glinting off the honeyed streaks that lit up the rich dark chocolate; it was terrifying how every cell in his body seemed to pull him towards her.

She stopped half a dozen times to take photographs, waiting for a clear shot, unexpectedly patient. He could have easily caught her, but he forced himself to wait, hold back. He was dangerously drawn to her and he needed to regain control of his senses before he joined her, spoke to her. Before she smiled at him.

He knew her scent, knew how her hand felt in his, knew exactly how perfectly she fit against him. He still had moments when the kiss they'd shared had come to him as strong as if it had only just happened. Moments when it had taken all his willpower not to reach for the phone and call her, just to hear the teasing note in her voice.

There had been no one since Eloise; he had wanted no one, but Alice Parker had caught him unawares.

She stopped to pick up a toy that an infant had dropped from its stroller, pausing to exchange a few words with the child's mother and the women shared a smile.

She was a disturbing distraction and he could not afford to be distracted. In spite of, or perhaps because of the way she had spilled out her worst moment under the stars at Combe St Philip, he did not entirely trust her.

Which didn't make sleeping any easier.

The market was coming to life and she stopped to look at some leather goods. Time to join her. He picked up a wallet.

'Fredrik . . . ' She hadn't looked around.

'Ally.'

She turned and looked up at him, not smiling, which should have been a relief but was anything but. 'How did you know where I was?' She held up a hand. 'Stupid question. The gate is monitored.'

'I had a message that one of our visitors had left the palace. I didn't have to ask who.'

'No . . . ' He'd expected a wry smile, was ready for it, but she merely shrugged and said, 'I'm sure Max and Flora are busy with the children but I wanted to take some photographs, get a feel for the place. Is that a problem?'

'Not at all, but the duty officer was concerned that you might get lost. Once you leave the square the little streets can become confusing.'

'How thoughtful, but you didn't have to come yourself,' she said, sorting through a stand containing belts. 'You could have sent a footman.'

She placed the faintest emphasis on the word footman.

His note had annoyed her?

'Footmen are household staff,' he said, holding back the smile that threatened. 'I could have sent one of my officers, of course, but I was concerned that you might be alarmed if you were approached by someone you did not know.'

'Oh.' She swallowed, her irritation dissolving in a moment. 'That was thoughtful. As was the car.' She finally turned to face him. 'Thank you, Fredrik.'

'You are a VIP this week, Ally,' he said, as if it had nothing to do with him. 'Are you going to buy anything?'

'These belts are lovely. I thought I'd buy one for my father.' She asked the price and the man, who clearly recognized him, reconsidered the tourist price he had been going to ask.

'What would you like to see?' he asked, as Ally, very happy with her bargain, paid and took her parcel.

'I don't know. What should I be looking at?'

'The statue of King Alonso?'

'Was he a good king?'

'No better and no worse than most but he fought a famous battle with a country that no longer exists.'

'So he won?'

'No, but he died with a sword in his hand, someone wrote a song about his bravery, folklore turned him into a hero and Alonso Day is a national holiday.'

'Not to be missed, then.'

He took her arm to guide her through the crowds that were filling the square, more social than shopping now. The busy stalls were serving coffee and snacks to young people gathering to sit at the tables. Mint tea to old men playing board games.

'Are you hungry?' he asked.

'A bit,' she admitted.

'There will be canapés at the reception, but it's going to be a long time until dinner.' He stopped at a stall, ordered coffee and deep-fried savoury pastries and then led her to a table. 'Alonso can wait.'

'I confess I'm not a huge fan of statues raised to leaders who take young men to war. There has to be a better way.'

'You'd think so but when tyrants threaten . . . ' Not wanting to prolong that conversation, he said, 'How are things going at Combe St Philip?'

'I've done as much as I can before the engagement announcement. I have the media package on my laptop for the local papers, ready to send the minute I have a photograph of Hope and Prince Jonas at the ball. I've also got a note for the vicar giving him all the details. I don't want him telling everyone that

Hope can't have the wedding that week because the church has been booked for a craft festival.'

'That's the cover story Max came up with?'

She grinned. 'He did good.'

'What about the village green party?'

'Hog roast booked. Carousel booked. Bouncy castle booked. I'll think of some more amusements before the day, but those are the big ones,' she said, reaching for her bag and taking out her tablet. 'Meanwhile I've prepared this.' She handed it across the table so that he could see the invitation she'd created. The background was a slightly faded-out image of the village green and the church. In large letters were the words 'Save the Day' and underneath, 'Your invitation to the Wedding on the Green'. The rest of the details — the who, the where, the when — were laid out in the briefest terms below.

'What are you going to do with it?' he asked, handing the tablet back to her.

'It's done. I've printed it out and

stuffed envelopes I've addressed personally to each householder in the village. They are safely tucked away in a box at the bottom of my wardrobe,' she said as their coffee and pastries arrived, 'and I have a draft email ready to send to mother after the announcement telling her what's going on and asking her to deliver the invitations personally that morning.'

'Getting to everyone before the press descend on the village?'

The hundred and fifty watt smile she gave him, his reward for getting it right, was like being struck by lightning. Fortunately, she picked up a pastry and bit into it with an appreciative moan, giving him a chance to get his breath back. 'This is so good.'

'It's a lot to ask of her,' he said, brushing the crumbs from his fingers for the sparrows hopping around their feet. 'Your mother.'

'You think? She'll knock on everyone's door so that she can hand over the invitation personally and share the best bit of news . . . ' There was a flake of pastry clinging to her lower lip . . . 'That I'm going to be Hope's bridesmaid.'

'Not a chore then, but a treat,' he said. 'Especially when she tells the landlady of the Three Bells.'

He was smiling he realized and Ally was smiling back and for a moment neither of them said anything.

She was the first to break eye contact, but there was an unexpected touch of colour on her cheekbones as she picked up her cup and took a sip of coffee.

It wasn't just him, then. She felt the connection too and he didn't know how he felt about that. It had been so long since he'd felt the familiar tug of heat, desire. So long. So unwanted.

'She also gets to tell her WI ladies that they are being asked to make the cakes for the Wedding on the Green,' Ally said. 'I've asked if they would be up to making cupcake posies for the tables. It's a challenge they will be unable to resist.'

'You have it all worked out.' Whatever he thought about her previous employment it was clear that Hope knew what she was doing when she'd asked Ally to take on the local PR. 'Who is paying for all this?' he asked. 'I know Max has insisted on paying for the wedding but he didn't bargain for the entire village.'

'No. Afterwards I felt rather guilty at adding to his burden so before I spoke to Hope, I asked Floradear if she thought it was too much.'

'Apparently not.'

She shook her head. 'Flora had already talked to Hope. She and Jonas thought it was a fun idea but Jonas insisted on paying for it. He's opened a credit card account for the Wedding on the Green with instructions that I spend whatever will make the day special. Marquee, hog roast, bouncy castle, all the fun of the fair.' She lifted an eyebrow. 'Do you have a problem with that?'

She was asking him if he still doubted her but if Jonas had asked his opinion he would have said to go ahead. The danger was not that she'd use his credit card to indulge her love of expensive shoes, but to his privacy.

'None whatsoever.' He checked the time. 'I hate to hurry you but we really should be getting back. Princess Anna won't hear about you escaping the palace from me, but if you're late for her reception we will all suffer.'

He stood up, thought about offering her his arm, decided against it and they walked, mostly in silence, back to the palace. Once there a footman stepped forward to show her to her room but she hadn't forgotten Fredrik's note and giving the man one of her luminous smiles, she said, 'Thank you, but I can find my own way.'

'Damn it, Ally . . . ' Fredrik dismissed the man with a glance, took her elbow and set off down the long corridor to the wing with the guest suites, not speaking, not saying anything until they reached her door.

He opened it. She walked through

and turned to face him. 'We always seem to be doing this. Maybe one day you'll come in.'

'I shouldn't even be here.'

'Why?' Then, with a little puff of irritation at her own obtuseness: 'Was it on that list of protocols sent with the invitation? No men in your room without the blessing of the church?'

'If you saw how far apart Princess Anna keeps Hope and Jonas you'd understand why they stay in London most of the time.'

'Really? Maybe that's why Hope looks . . . '

'What?'

'Edgy?'

'Undoubtedly,' he said. 'Oh, what the hell . . . ' He stepped through the door, shut it behind him and took her face in his hands. No surprise this time, no shocked reaction as he slowly lowered his mouth to her waiting lips, watching every flicker of expression, the quick flush of pink across her cheekbones. He saw her eyes darken, the flicker of her lashes as they lowered, heard the little sigh as their lips met in a gentle, exploratory kiss.

It was as different from that first shockingly unexpected kiss as it could be. A question. A promise ... A kiss that could have lasted forever but time was running out and he drew back.

'I'll see you later, Miss Parker.'

'Yes, sir,' she replied, her voice soft as silk velvet, her eyes still closed and it was only the knowledge that if he kissed her again they would both be in trouble that kept him backing away.

★ ★ ★

Ally stood, eyes closed, for a long minute after Fredrik had gone. Reliving his touch, every moment of that kiss until she was roused by a light tap on the door.

She took a long slow breath, opened her eyes, said, 'Come in.'

It was the maid with her dress.

7

Ally saw Fredrik long before he saw her. He was talking to someone and they both had their backs to her. Both men were wearing dinner jackets, broad shoulders displayed to perfection by the black broadcloth. One was dark, the other had light brown frosted hair that was still damp from the shower.

As she left the carpet and her heels clicked on the marble floor Fredrik half turned and for a moment seemed lost for words. For a long while they just looked at one another, the memory of that slow kiss in his eyes, in the tingle that rippled through her body.

Realizing that he no longer had Fredrik's attention, the other man turned. He too looked and then his face lit up in a broad smile. 'Ally! What a relief.' He crossed to her and taking her by the shoulders kissed both her cheeks. 'You have saved my evening.'

'Prince Nico . . . ' Really? Of all the dozens of women he must have met in the last couple of years he remembered her? 'I can't believe you remember me.'

Fredrik, momentarily frozen, glanced from Nico to her. 'You've met?'

'At a charity dinner in London, Fredrik. Ally was there, taking photographs, talking to people. She stopped at our table for a while and brightened an otherwise deadly evening.'

'I have no doubt, but tonight she is going to brighten mine,' he replied, taking her arm in what could only be described as a possessive gesture. 'Princess Anna's orders. My reward for good behaviour,' he added, pointedly.

Ally should have been outraged but she was too interested in the by-play between the two men to care.

Nico pulled a face. 'That woman has plans to marry me off to some Gorgon.'

Realizing that Fredrik could not comment on either the Crown Princess or her choice of a suitable wife for

Nico, Ally said, 'It must be sooo tough being a prince.'

'Not that tough, *cara*. I outrank a count.' His grin was full of mischief. 'I will see you later.'

Fredrik said something to Nico in a language that Ally didn't understand. His eyebrows rose and, raising his hands, he backed off.

'What did you say to him?' she asked, as Fredrik took her arm and led her up a seemingly endless flight of wide marble steps.

'I just reminded him that this evening is not about him,' Fredrik said, 'and in case you were tempted to risk the lightning I should warn you that the Crown Princess has other plans for Nico.'

'The Gorgon?'

'That's just Nico being childish. She's a fine woman and if she can be persuaded to take him on she'll be the making of him.'

'I'm glad to hear it. Nico is sweet, but indiscreet. If I'd used any of the gossip he told me while plying me with champagne, I'd have got a bonus and he would have been barred from at least two of his favourite nightclubs.'

'You didn't use what he told you?'

'I never considered it my job to ruin people — an attitude on which the new editor of *Celebrity* and I chose to differ. Nico is unhappy, Fredrik, but he needs to grow up and find a purpose in life before he becomes a permanent fixture on the covers of gossip magazines.'

Ahead of them footmen leapt to open a pair of ten-foot-high double doors and Nico's future was forgotten as Fredrik led her into the state drawing room.

'Oh my . . . '

Ally had been determined not to appear overwhelmed by the grandeur of the palace but the state drawing room was jaw-dropping in its magnificence.

The walls were covered in cream and gold figured silk, the windows swagged with heavy green brocade and half a dozen crystal chandeliers picked out the gilded and painted plasterwork on the ceiling.

As if that wasn't enough, tall windows overlooked immaculately sculptured gardens, which had been lit to reveal intricate knotwork, marble statues tucked into niches and an elaborate fountain on which mythical gods rode dolphins spewing water that sparkled in the lights.

It wasn't a room in which you were going to sit down and put your feet up; it was a room created to impress and it did. Totally.

Fredrik stopped a passing footman, took two glasses of champagne and handed one to her. It took a will of iron not to swig it straight down and take another. Instead she took a sip then put it on the nearest available surface as Fredrik introduced her to a royal cousin.

She began to relax as they small-talked their way around the room, Ally conscious only of Fredrik at her side, the obvious respect in which everyone held him.

'Ally . . . ' She turned as Hope joined them, gave her a hug. 'The Crown Princess has asked to meet you.'

Ally swallowed. Working a cocktail party was what she did — had done — for a living, but this was different and she was ridiculously glad to feel Fredrik's hand in the small of her back as Hope led the way to the icy pale, scarily slender Crown Princess. The slightly less scary Crown Prince smiled at her.

Fredrik presented her and she pulled off the curtsey bob that she'd practised without wobbling on her heels.

'Your Serene Highness . . . '

'Miss Parker . . . ' Princess Anna gave her a long, cool look, assessing her clothes, judging them. Was the dress too sexy? The V-neck too plunging? 'Did you have a good journey?'

'Yes, thank you, ma'am.'

'And you have everything you need?'

'Yes, ma'am.' She wasn't allowed to ask a direct question so this could be a very stilted and one-sided conversation unless she took the initiative. 'I took a walk into the city early this evening. I was hoping to see the statue of King

Alonso but I ran out of time.'

'I do hope you were not alone.'

'No, ma'am. Count Fredrik was kind enough to escort me.'

She nodded, apparently satisfied. 'I understand that you are creating a wedding diary for Miss Kennard? It will be — ' she searched for a word to express her reservations ' — fitting, I hope.'

'I have some sample pages on my tablet, ma'am,' she replied. 'I brought them to show Hope, but if you could spare a few minutes tomorrow, I would be happy to show you what I have in mind.' Realizing that the Crown Princess could veto the whole idea if she didn't approve, that she needed her onside, she added, 'I would welcome any comments.'

'My secretary will call you in the morning.' She turned to Fredrik. 'What entertainment have you arranged for Miss Parker, Count?'

'A little sightseeing tomorrow, lunch in one of the restaurants in the harbour.'

'You aren't taking her to see your mountains?'

There was the slightest pause before Prince Carlo intervened. 'It will be very cold at this time of year, Anna.' He turned to her. 'You must come back in the summer, Miss Parker. We can arrange a picnic in one the alpine meadows.'

'Thank you, sir.'

Dismissed, they returned to the party and she would have been hard put to say which of them was the most relieved to escape but when, instinctively, she put out her hand, Fredrik took it, held it tightly for a moment. He was about to say something when an elegant, dark-haired woman approached them.

'Celina . . . '

He released her hand to greet the woman warmly with a kiss on both cheeks, one of his rare smiles.

'Hello, Fredrik, how are you?'

Celina's accent was unexpectedly American but then she remembered Hope telling her that the formidable Dowager Princess had an American social secretary.

'Celina, may I introduce Alice Parker?

Ally, Celina Harris.'

'Hi, Ally, I've heard all about you from Hope. I'm sorry to drag you away but the Dowager Princess has asked to meet you.'

'I think I'm supposed to say that I'm honoured but frankly, I'm terrified.'

Celina laughed, exchanged a glance with Fredrik, then said, 'Right answer. Are you coming, Fredrik?'

'I wouldn't miss it.'

They clearly knew each other well. It was to be expected. They both worked in the palace, probably saw each other every day and were friends. More? Ally found herself having to contain a spasm of something very much like jealousy as they walked towards the sofa where Her Serene Highness, the Dowager Princess Margaret, was holding court. This time Ally missed the comfort of Fredrik's reassuring hand at her back.

'Your Highness, may I present Miss Alice Parker. You will recall that she is going to be one of Hope's bridesmaids.'

Ally repeated her curtsey.

'Another giraffe,' the Dowager said, grumpily. 'What on earth do they feed girls these days?' Not expecting an answer, she said, 'Oh, well, I suppose you'll be a match for that other girl but for goodness' sake sit down so I don't have to crane my neck to look at you.'

Ally sat and the Princess waved Celina and Fredrik away.

'You work for one of those gossip magazines I understand,' she said, getting straight to the point. 'Are we going to see candid photographs of the wedding party all over the media?'

'No, Your Highness. I haven't worked for *Celebrity* for several months, but I have no doubt Prince Jonas will be approached by all the major lifestyle magazines with a generous offer for exclusive coverage of the wedding.'

'They are not film stars.'

'No, and Hope has already told me that they both want the wedding to be a private, family affair.'

'So what's all this nonsense I hear about a diary?'

'The diary is about Hope's journey,' she replied, patiently. 'It's provisionally entitled *Becoming a Princess*.' Hope hated it — becoming a princess was the last thing she wanted — but she'd accepted that it would grab the interest of the media, which would help it to sell. 'Princess Anna has kindly agreed to take a look at some pages I've prepared and offer her comments.'

'Don't think you can get anything sleazy past her,' the Dowager warned.

'I'm doing this for a woman I've known since I was three years old, ma'am. Who is one of my very best friends.' She was getting very tired of having to defend herself to everyone. 'I would do nothing to hurt her.'

'One of them. How many 'best friends' do you have?'

'Two. I believe you have already met Flora Deare.'

'Who is also getting married. It seems Miss Parker that you going to be the perennial bridesmaid.'

Flora was marrying Max? Ally glanced

across the room at Flora, who seemed a little flushed. At Max, who looked . . . He was looking at Flora and there was absolutely no doubt what he was thinking.

'Yes,' she said, grinning. 'And I couldn't be more pleased.' She took a breath. 'Maybe I could show you the diary pages too, ma'am?'

'Maybe. I'll think about it,' she said, making a gesture.

Celina and Fredrik, who she had seen talking together, just out of the corner of her eye, reappeared, and aware that she'd been dismissed Ally stood up and repeated her curtsey. 'Thank you, ma'am.'

'How did that go?' Fredrik asked but before she could answer there was a general movement. Some people made their farewells while those who remained made their way through to the dining room.

'I'm surprised you weren't partnered with Celina for this gig,' Ally said. 'You seem to get on well.'

'Princess Margaret needs her.' He glanced at her. 'We did go out a couple of times, a concert, dinner, but there was no chemistry.'

'Really? I would have thought you were perfectly suited,' she said, as if it mattered not a jot. It shouldn't. This, whatever this was, wasn't going anywhere. At best it could be an interesting fling but there was a warm ache tempting her to step up and take a ride on the roundabout.

'I agree. It should have worked,' Fredrik replied. 'On paper it was perfect. We have a lot in common, we're good friends, but Celina isn't over her ex and I'm . . . ' He shrugged.

'What?' she prompted, but they were at the entrance to the dining room and the moment passed as Fredrik checked the seating plan.

When he turned away, took her arm, it was if she was looking at a different man. He hadn't been smiling before but now his face was expressionless, his eyes shuttered as he escorted her to her seat then, without a word, took his own place on the far side of the table. Flora and Max were both miles away, as were Hope and Jonas. There was nothing to do but turn to the man on her right and introduce herself. And she found herself looking at a face she knew.

She glanced at the card in front him. Fit Lt the Hon Dominic Jensson.

Fredrik's brother?

She looked across at Fredrik but his attention had been claimed by Princess Anna's sister, Lady Katya, who was seated to his right.

'How is my big brother?' Dominic asked, following her gaze. 'I wouldn't ask but our mother worries about him.' When she turned to look at him he held out his hand. 'Dominic Jensson.'

'Alice Parker. Ally . . . ' Her first thought, that if his mother was worried she should call him, died unspoken. Fredrik hadn't introduced her to his brother even though he'd been standing right beside him. Hadn't acknowledged him. 'I'm afraid I don't know Fredrik well enough to comment on his health,' she said.

She realized that while she'd opened up to Fredrik, all he'd told her about himself was that he'd suffered from posttraumatic stress disorder and he'd only done that to persuade her to talk. She didn't know him at all.

'You don't?' He seemed surprised. 'I thought, hoped . . . ' He coloured a little. 'I was told that you seemed close.'

Told? By who? 'I didn't see you at the reception,' she said.

'I've only just come off duty. Barely had time to scramble into the penguin suit. I don't usually get invited to palace dos. They must be a man down.'

'I understand the Crown Princess is very hot on keeping things tidy,' she said.

'A bit of stickler . . . sergeant major type.' Ally smiled and encouraged he said, 'How is he?'

'Why doesn't your mother ask him, herself?'

'She would if he would see her, answer her calls. She sat at his bedside, holding his hand, praying for him, when he was injured. When we thought he would lose his leg but once he was conscious . . . '

Fredrik didn't see his mother? Didn't talk to her?

Ally tried to imagine what it must be like to have a son come home from a war zone with the possibility of life-changing injuries. A son you couldn't hold, comfort . . .

Dominic was being incredibly indiscreet considering they'd only just met. Or angry. Or maybe just desperate.

Was it coincidence that she had been seated next to him?

'What happened?' she asked, hoping to draw him out.

'He was on a UN peacekeeping mission. You know the drill, observe, be neutral, don't get involved, but a school was in the way. He went in, got the kids out. The head count was one short and he'd gone back to look for the missing child when a rocket hit the building. Total bloody hero . . . '

Yes there was anger, but he was desperate enough to reach out to a stranger who might, just might, be able to reach him.

'What about the child?' she asked.

He shook his head and she looked across at Fredrik. The narrow silk ribbon on his lapel was public recognition of his bravery but that one failure must surely haunt him.

He was talking to Lady Katya, but as if he felt her eyes on him he looked up, his face all shadows in the flickering candlelight.

She wanted to go to him, put her arms around him, comfort him, but he turned away.

'You can see how he is,' she said to Dominic. 'There's scarcely any suggestion of a limp.'

'His body healed.'

The statement was loaded with a mute appeal but she ignored the invitation to discuss Fredrik's state of mind. 'You're wearing wings so I'm guessing you're a pilot,' she said. 'Army? Air force?'

'Army,' he replied, relieved — she

thought — at the firm change of subject. 'It's the family business. Long story.'

He grinned so easily but then he was younger than his brother, hadn't heard the sound of an inbound shell, failed to save the life of a child.

'Why don't you tell me the short version,' she suggested.

'It all started with a multi-times great-grandfather who stowed away on a cargo vessel leaving Denmark. Details are sketchy but it seems he had been serving his master's wife in more ways than one and he had to flee for his life.'

Denmark? That fit Fredrik's Nordic colouring. His name.

'How did he end up here?' she asked.

'When he was discovered by the crew he was put to work on basic rations and the first chance he got he jumped ship. San Michele was at war with one of their neighbours and, penniless, he signed on as a mercenary.' He paused as a plate was placed in front of him. 'Didn't Fredrik tell you any of this?'

'I told you, I barely know him. We've

been paired by Princess Anna because we were both spares. She likes things tidy.' She picked up a fork but, no longer hungry, began to toy with something pretty on her plate. 'It's a bit of a leap from mercenary to Count. Where did the title come from?'

'He saved the life of the Crown Prince, carrying him from the battle-field despite his own wounds. He was a rogue, but he didn't lack courage. He was feted as a hero and taken to the palace to recover where he reverted to type and seduced one of the younger, more impressionable princesses.'

'He lived dangerously.'

Dominic laughed. 'You're right. Under normal circumstances he would have been executed and the pregnant princess would have been sent to a convent to hide her shame. But he'd been proclaimed a national hero at a time when the country needed heroes and a royal wedding is always good PR, so a priest was summoned, our heroic ancestor was given a title and they lived, so the story goes, happily ever after.'

'*Ex fortitudine patria* . . . Out of courage, a country.'

Dominic grinned. 'He was a total chancer but the Jenssons have served the royal family ever since.'

'Do they have to sacrifice more than one son?' she asked, thinking of the mother who had seen one son badly wounded. A son who wouldn't answer her calls.

'No, but all I ever wanted to do was fly. Suzanna has joined the diplomatic service. Katerina and Alessandro are still at school, but Alessandro has already decided he wants to be an architect, like his father.' Catching her questioning look he said, 'Our father died when Fredrik was eleven. He was never the same afterwards. Never really with us and when Mother remarried three years later . . . ' He looked across the table. 'He's never forgiven her for that.'

Anger, desperation and a hurt he was too young to hide.

★ ★ ★

Fredrik exchanged the usual pleasant-
ries with Lady Katya, but his mind was
totally fixed on Ally. He could feel her
questioning eyes on him but the shock
of seeing Dominic's name on the table
plan had wiped all the basic courtesies
from his mind.

What on earth was he doing here
and sitting next to Ally? This was an
occasion for the closest family and
advisors . . .

He glanced at the Dowager, who'd
been a close friend of his grandmother's, suspecting that she'd had a hand
in this. He anticipated an answering
challenge, but she was talking to Max
and either didn't notice his look, or
chose not to.

His gaze was drawn back to Ally.

'Hope's friend is lovely,' Lady Katya
said.

'Yes,' he said. 'Yes, she is.' When she
walked across the palace lobby towards
him he thought his heart had stopped.

She was wearing a dress in some soft, clinging fabric that draped around her, hugging her figure. A silver pendant rested just above a hint of cleavage and her legs were accentuated by a pair of heels so high, so slender, that it was a wonder they could support her.

She had twisted her hair up, fastening it with a silver and turquoise pin. It looked as if all it would take was one tug to have it all tumbling around her shoulders and, God help him, that was all he'd wanted to do all evening.

'Would you like me to change places with her, Fredrik?' she asked, laughing.

Yes . . . 'No.' It was too late. She was already deep in conversation with his brother and would be hearing all the things he should have told her from his brother's point of view. 'Thank you, ma'am, but while you might be brave enough to mess with your sister's seating plan, I am not.'

He made an attempt at civilized conversation, asking after her children, but he could hear Ally laughing at something the man on her right had said to her.

At least it wasn't Nico. He was further up the table flirting like mad with Flora who appeared to be flirting back with rather more enthusiasm than you'd expect from a recently engaged woman.

Ally wasn't flirting. She was being the perfect dinner guest: attentive, charming as she engaged with those around her. Ignoring her wine glass in favour of water. If her plan was to keep her wits about her in the hope of picking up gossip, she would have been well rewarded. Not that *Celebrity* would be interested in his miserable story.

For a moment he caught her eye; she did not look away, clearly waiting for something, anything by way of response from him. He had nothing, merely the endless emptiness that had only disappeared high in the mountains until he'd met her. He had never been more relieved to see Prince Carlo rise to his feet to say a few words of welcome to their guests from England.

He was mercifully brief. The moment he had finished, Princess Anna stood, a signal for the women to leave the room.

He watched Ally leave, then turned to his brother, wondering what he'd said to her. But while he'd been watching Ally, Dominic had slipped away through the door that led to the lift down to the kitchens. No doubt the way he had arrived.

When they joined the women in the white drawing room, Ally and Hope were settled on a sofa, deep in conversation, then Flora buttonholed her. Ignoring the coffee — he was already so wired that he would find it hard to sleep — he went straight for the brandy.

Max eventually led away a slightly unsteady Flora and when Ally put down the cup she was holding and made to follow them he made his move.

'Ally . . . '

'Fredrik.'

Her smile barely reached her eyes,

her voice was cool and instead of the apology he'd been mentally rehearsing, he heard himself say, 'Why do you call yourself that when you have such a lovely name?'

He thought for a moment that she wasn't going to answer. That she was simply waiting for him to move out of her way but then she said, 'Alice is what my mother called me when I was sick as a kid and she sat all night by my bed. She said it softly, over and over, like a prayer. It's what she called me when I was naughty. Al-ice!' She was speaking softly, but that unmistakable rising intonation of a furious mother came through. ''Oh, *Alice*!' is what she says when I've disappointed her.' She made a tiny moue. 'When, rarely, I've made her proud. She's earned that right. No one else.' She waited. 'Is that it?'

'What did Dominic say to you?'

'That you don't talk to your mother. That she sat by your bed and prayed when you were injured. That you sent her away when you were strong enough to say the words.'

'I didn't send her away. I sensed her there but when I finally came out of it, she had gone.'

'She knew you wouldn't want her there?' She was clearly horrified. Anyone would be. 'Because she remarried?'

'Yes . . . ' It was what everyone thought. They thought him distant, cruel and he hadn't cared because anything was better than the truth. Now Ally would think it and she, too, would walk away. But this time it was different. As he looked at her he realized that he would do anything to change that and he said, 'No.'

And just as she had when Princess Anna suggested a trip into the mountains, she reached out and took his hand.

8

Fredrik looked down at their hands, then up at her as if unsure what to say or do. Ally wasn't sure, either, only that he'd known when she needed to talk. Now she felt the same need in him and no matter how bad it was, she would be there. She would listen. She would do her best not to judge.

'Walk me to my room, Fredrik.'

For a moment she thought he was going to make excuses, go through the whole protocol thing again, but then his grasp tightened and he walked her out of the white drawing room, past a blank-faced footman and down the seemingly endless corridors without a word.

She didn't wait for him to do his 'gentleman' bit but pushed the door open, drawing him in after her, closing it.

'I went to see him,' she said, before he could speak. 'The boy in the car park.'

If the sudden switch in subject threw him he didn't show it. He was showing nothing . . . Then he said, 'On your own?'

'He's an accountant. Very respectable.' Her hand still in his, she turned and walked across to a sofa set before the fireplace, only letting go to kick off her shoes and curl up into the corner of the sofa. He bent, lit the gas fire but when he joined her on the sofa he kept a safe distance. 'He has an office in Ayesborough,' she said. 'The day after you left I phoned and made an appointment.'

'Did he know it was you?'

'I gave his receptionist my name and address. He was expecting me.'

Fredrik, concentrating on her story now, lifted his knee to the cushion and turned to face her. 'What did he say?'

'Nothing.' She swallowed, remembering the shock of it. 'He just stood there looking at me, tears running down his cheeks.'

'He was afraid you were going to make trouble?'

'No.' It hadn't been like that. 'They were tears of relief, I think. The chance to finally apologize, explain.'

'He could have done that any time in the last few years.'

'It's hard, though, isn't it? It would have taken a lot more courage than he had to walk up to my front door and knock. To get past my mother. And the longer you wait, the harder it becomes.'

Fredrik managed a half-smile. 'She disapproved of his sister, I recall. Your mother.'

'She disapproved of the whole family.'

'With good reason.'

She shrugged, acknowledging the truth of that. 'She has high standards.'

'She's a good mother. You're very lucky.'

'Yes.' She knew it and her heart broke for whatever had happened between him and his own mother.

'So what did this respectable accountant have to say for himself?'

'It seems that he'd overheard his sister talking on the phone. She and her little clique planned to get me drunk and, once I was sufficiently out of it, the boys were going to be invited to draw lots to do me the favour of relieving me of my virginity.' She pulled a face so that he wouldn't see her shiver. 'My stupid fault for thinking I could — '

'You were not to blame, Ally,' he said, sharply. 'They were jealous of both you and Hope. You had something that they would never have.' She raised a questioning eyebrow. 'A future.'

'Yes, well, I realize that now but teenage girls are desperate for a tribe. To be part of the group.' She shook her head. 'Simon told her that he knew what she planned, that he was going to tell their mother. She just laughed, but said I was a stuck-up cow not worth bothering with, that leaving me waiting all night in the Three Bells car park would bring me down a peg or two.'

'And he began to think about that.'

'He came to tell me to go home.'

'But there you were, waiting in the dark. He was already churned up, excited to be your hero, his teenage hormones out of control.'

'He said he was so nervous he couldn't speak and reached out without thinking and when I screamed he panicked. Afterwards he wanted to come and tell me he was sorry but he couldn't face me and the longer he waited the more impossible it got. The years slip by and it's still there, for both you. A dark place in the mind where you never go.' She looked across at Fredrik, wanting him to understand what she was saying. That it was never too late . . .

The room fell silent. Outside, a sentry's footsteps echoed along the castle battlements. A car with a hole in its exhaust growled up the hill. A ferry hooted as it arrived in the port.

Fredrik understood what Ally had been doing. She was showing him how talking, confronting something bad that had happened to her, had made the fear, the darkness, go away and he was glad to have been a small part of that.

'What did Dominic tell you?' he asked again. 'Apart from the fact that I don't speak to my mother.'

'Isn't that enough?' He didn't answer. 'He said that you never forgave her for marrying again. For moving on, having a life, being happy when your father was dead.' She tilted her head and a curl escaped the pin, descended to her shoulder. She pushed it behind her ear. 'You're saying that's not true?'

He shook his head. 'It's part of it, I suppose, and I let people think it, especially my brother and sister, because it's easier for them.'

He'd never told a soul what had happened and he could stop now, get up, walk away. It was what he'd been doing all his life. From his mother, from his family, from Eloise. He'd watched Ally this evening, talking to Dominic, talking to her friends, knowing that this moment would come and tried to convince himself that it didn't matter because he scarcely knew her. A couple of kisses, a walk in the dark, a cup of coffee in the square. It should have meant nothing.

Should have.

He'd spent very little time with Ally but for every moment of it she had challenged him, laughed at him, laughed with him, teased him and made him feel alive. He'd arrived in Combe St Philip determined not to trust her further than he could throw her. She might be Hope's best friend, but she didn't have a job or any prospect of one and he knew exactly how much she owed on her credit cards.

Common sense told him that she had to be building a story around the royal wedding. It had everything. The scandal involving the bride's father. The protocol-mad Crown Princess who'd had an empathy bypass and was having entire litters of kittens at the idea of a royal wedding taking place in an English village, completely out of her control. She already knew the younger playboy prince with his string of B-minus celebrity girlfriends, who the family were trying to marry off to The Gorgon. Nico would be only too happy to offload to a friendly ear. And then there was the palace head of security who suffered from PTSD and was estranged from his family.

Celebrity, or one of its rivals, having had their offers of seven-figure sums for exclusive coverage of the wedding turned down by Hope and Jonas, would doubtless pay a fortune to be able to run that story the week of the wedding. It would triple their circulation.

Best friends had been betrayed for a lot less and yet every instinct told him that she was the real deal.

The silence had gone on for an age but she had not rushed him, had waited for him to decide whether to open up or walk away; bare his soul or leave without a backward glance.

He knew that if he held out his hand she would take it, wanting to make it easier for him but there could be no attempt to soften the story, to win her empathy through touch. Just the bare, cold truth.

He focused on an ornate ormolu clock sitting on the mantel. A fat cherub . . . 'When I was eleven years old,' be began, his mouth as dry as if he'd run a four-minute mile, 'I saw my mother kill my father.'

He heard the little puff of shock that she had been unable to contain.

'I wasn't supposed to be there. My father had been climbing with a friend when he fell off the rock-face. He'd had a heart attack. The rope saved him from more than cuts and grazes. If he'd been at home, or in his office, he would have been in the emergency room within minutes, recovery pretty much assured, but by the time the mountain rescue team reached him he was in a coma. He was in hospital for a while and then my mother had him brought home.'

Everything was as sharp and clear as the day it had happened.

'I was supposed to be in school but I knew something was wrong so I bunked off, wanting to be with him. I arrived just in time to see my mother switch off his life support system.'

'Fredrik . . . '

'I watched for a moment, not sure, but then the machine monitoring his heartbeat began to stutter and a moment later the room was filled with that high-pitched sound as it flatlined.'

He turned from the cherub to look at her. Her eyes were streaming with tears and without thinking he moved to gather her in and, as he breathed into her hair, felt her warmth, he wanted to weep, too.

'I'm sorry. I shouldn't have told you.'

'You needed to tell someone. I'm glad you trusted me enough . . . ' She gave a little sniff. 'What did you do?'

'I backed away, went back to school . . . ' He took a long breath. 'A little while later the headmaster came to find me, told me that my father had died. That I was the man of the family and it was my duty to support my mother, take care of Dominic and Katerina.'

And that's what he'd done, she realized. Protected his mother and his younger siblings from what he'd seen, but at a terrible cost to himself.

'Have you ever talked to anyone about this?'

'I found it difficult to talk to my mother. At first it was put down to grief though eventually I was sent to a see a child psychologist but what was I going to say? That my mother had murdered my father?' He stood up, turned away, his arm on the mantel as he stared down into the flames of the gas fire.

'You've never told anyone? A family member, a priest?'

He shook his head and her heart just about broke for that eleven-year-old boy who'd seen something he didn't understand. The man whose mind was frozen in that moment of trauma and who had been protecting his mother ever since. Protecting her, but unable to forgive her.

What on earth could she say to him? How could she help him?

She stood up, went to him, took his hands in hers.

'Fredrik, you were a child. Someone should have talked to you, helped you understand what had happened.'

His jaw clenched. 'I saw what happened.'

'You saw the moment your mother switched off the life support machine but ask yourself what had happened in the days before that. Ask yourself why your mother had your father brought home. Ask the doctor who cared for him; ask to see his notes. Better still,' she said, 'go and ask your mother.' She raised herself on tiptoes and kissed his cheek. 'Do it now.'

★　★　★

Ally had lain awake for hours, haunted by the boy who'd lost his father so young and had never come to terms with it. Haunted by the look on Fredrik's face

173

as he'd turned, grey-faced, and walked from her room without a word.

He'd opened an emotional artery but instead of offering him unconditional comfort, taking him to her bed, she'd told him to think about what he'd seen. Not through the eyes of that eleven-year-old boy but as an adult.

She was sure that she was right that, stuck in the groundhog-day loop of trauma, he had never been able to see that his father was in a vegetative state, that the medical staff had left his mother to say her last goodbye in private before doing this one last thing for the man she loved.

Would he be able to see that truth or was he too locked in to his nightmare? She should have followed him. Would have but for the sharp click as he'd closed the door that made it very clear that he wanted to be alone.

She understood, but knew that if the situation had been reversed nothing would have deterred him. He would have followed her, made sure that she came to no harm. Not that he needed protecting, except perhaps from himself.

Dominic had placed a card into her hand as she'd left the table. She'd put it in the little clutch bag she'd been carrying without a glance but now, unable to sleep, she thought she might ring him. Tell him what had happened. Ask him to go and look for his brother.

There was just a name, Claudia Nero, and a telephone number printed on the front. On the back she had written, 'I'm Fredrik's mother. Please call me.'

Despite the lateness of the hour she had no doubt that her call would be picked up before the second ring — but what could she say?

She'd already said more than enough and pulling a sweater and pants over her PJs and grabbing her phone, she ran along the corridor. She'd half expected to see a footman standing in the grand marble and gilt entrance, but there was no one there. The doors were shut; well of course they were, and not just shut. A light blinking on and off warned her that an alarm had replaced the sentries. Had she set it off? Was there a hidden camera? She looked around, wondering if Fredrik was in his office, if he could see her. If one of his men would come and politely escort her back to her room.

No one came and, afraid that she would wake the whole palace and embarrass Fredrik if she tried to open the door, she walked back to her room. Leaving the door unlocked in case he returned, she curled up on the sofa, certain that she would not sleep. But the sofa was huge, the cushions soft; it had been a very long day and the next thing she knew it was daylight.

Horrified that she'd fallen asleep when Fredrik was out there somewhere, feeling heaven knew what, she reached for her phone hoping for a message, something, anything to reassure her.

There was nothing. Determined to go and find him she threw back the cover and headed for the bathroom. She had taken two, maybe three steps, when she stopped, turned . . .

She hadn't taken a blanket from the bed.

It had to have been Fredrik. Who else could it have been?

He'd come back, found her asleep and covered her up. She looked around, saw a note propped against a bowl of flowers.

It wasn't a card in one of his crested envelopes. It was just a sheet of lined paper torn from a small pocket notebook and it said, 'Lunch, 12.30. F'

She swallowed, felt the prick of tears against her lids as relief flooded through her.

The note was brusque and he'd already told Prince Carlo that he was taking her to lunch so this might just be duty. But he was safe.

She crossed to the window and threw it open, breathing in the soft, salt-laden air.

The sea was milky calm with a mist

that was turning gold in the sunrise. It was too beautiful to be inside and she pulled on a vest and shorts and tied back her hair and went for a heart-pumping run around the battlements.

She finally stopped to do her cooling-down exercise, took a swig from the water bottle she carried and leaned against the parapet. There were layers of sound: the murmur of voices, birds proclaiming territorial rights, the hoot of a ferry arriving in the port. She stowed them all away to bring out later when she wrote about San Michele.

Back in her room she took a shower, then spent some time choosing what to wear.

Protocol suggested she needed to wear something very grown-up to call on the Crown Princess and the Dowager, but she didn't want to look like a journalist. She wanted to look like Hope's friend.

She settled on a pair of bright pink capri pants, a fine short-sleeved cotton sweater and a pair of pink and white polka dot high-heeled sandals. They were girlfriend casual and exactly what she'd choose to wear for a waterfront lunch with a good-looking man. The shoes might even make him smile.

Luisa brought tea, warm croissants wrapped in a napkin and fresh orange juice while Ally was painting her toenails to match her shoes.

Obviously surprised to see her up and dressed Luisa said, 'Madam Flora is still fast asleep. Sir Max is with the children.'

She sounded a touch disapproving and Ally looked up, smiled. 'They are his children, Luisa. Is Miss Hope about?'

'I have not seen her.'

She wanted to ask if she'd seen Fredrik. If he was in his office, but restrained herself.

She finished her nails, ate her breakfast and had just got dressed when her phone rang. The number came up as 'not recognized'. Not Fredrik.

'Ally Parker,' she said.

'Thank you . . . ' The woman's voice

was soft, her English faintly accented. 'I don't know what you said to Fredrik but thank you.'

'Signora Nero?'

'Claudia, please.'

'How was he?' she asked.

'It was difficult,' she admitted. 'For both of us. We had not spoken for so long. It will take time . . . ' She gave a little sob. 'If I'd known what he'd seen I would have tried to explain that there was nothing left of his father. Only a shell kept alive by machines. Otto knew the risks he took and he'd made a living will.'

'Did you show him?'

'Yes, but I should have talked to Fredrik about what was going to happen. I thought he was too young to understand. I thought it would be simpler . . . I did not have the courage.'

'No one knows how to handle something like this, Claudia. Was there no one there to support you?'

'Otto's parents were old and would not have understood. My family live in

Italy. Alessandro wanted to be there but it did not seem appropriate.'

Alessandro? That was her youngest son's name . . .

'Signor Nero?' she queried.

'He was Otto's best friend. They were climbing together when he fell. There was nothing he could have done, but he still felt responsible.'

So his mother hadn't just remarried, she'd married the man who was with her husband when he fell. No wonder people assumed that was the reason Fredrik couldn't forgive her. She was sure that Claudia Nero was a lovely woman, but there was, perhaps, something a little shaky in her judgement.

'It will get better, Claudia,' she assured her. 'Give it time.'

'Will you come and see me, Ally?'

Oh, good grief. Not without talking to Fredrik first. 'I'm fully booked until after lunch and I'm not sure what the palace have planned, Claudia. Can I call you?'

'Of course.'

$\star$ $\star$ $\star$

Ally tapped on Hope's door and the moment it was opened she was enveloped in a huge hug. 'I've hardly had a moment to talk to you. Last night was an endless round of Jonas's uncles, aunts and cousins come to inspect me.'

'Did you pass?'

'Who knows,' she said. 'You'd think I was marrying the entire royal family.' She shrugged. 'I suppose I am. But forget them. How are you coping with the desperately dour Count? I tried to talk Princess Anna out of pairing him up with you. You're going to be stuck with him here and at the wedding and you'll be bored to death.'

'I promise you I haven't been bored one moment in his company and he's taking me somewhere down by the harbour for lunch. Do you think these will put a smile on his face?' she asked, waggling a toe of her pink polka dot sandal.

Hope laughed. 'He'd be made of

wood if they didn't.'

'He's definitely not made of wood.'

'Oh?' Hope's eyes widened. 'Tell me more.'

Ally gave her a blow-by-blow description of their first meeting until they were both laughing but then Hope's smiled faded and she seemed to be somewhere else entirely.

'Are you okay, Hope?'

'What? Oh, yes . . . It's just that all this is a bit much.' She made a gesture that took in the palace and everything in it but before Ally could push it she said, 'Let's have a look at your ideas for the diary.'

'Okay. Do you want the good news or the bad news?'

'What's the bad news?'

'It's going to be called *Becoming a Princess*.'

Hope groaned. 'I don't want to be a wretched princess. You've met Anna . . . '

'One, Anna is the Crown Princess and has a lot on her shoulders. Two, the title is commercial. It does what it says on the tin and it will sell like hotcakes.'

Hope sighed. 'I trust your judgement, Al, and if we're going to do this we have to go for it whole-heartedly. So what's the good news?'

'I've shown it to the Crown Princess and the Dowager. I had a summons first thing and they met me together, prepared to gang up on me I suspect if it didn't meet with their approval. In the event they seemed pleasantly surprised. They even promised a quote.'

'About how much they were looking forward to the wedding?'

'Who knows, but Prince Carlo popped in, took a look and asked if it was a women-only thing or could he tell the world how happy you've made Jonas.'

'What? Oh . . . '

Rather than flattered, Hope look flattened and concerned.

Ally reached out and took her hand. 'Forget Jonas. How happy are you?'

Hope sighed. 'I'm not sure that love makes you happy, Al.' She looked out of the window as if desperate to escape.

'Maybe it's just weddings and receptions and balls that are the problem. Or Crown Princesses with a protocol fixation.' She pulled a face, attempting to make a joke of it. 'Ignore me. I'm suffering from a surfeit of footmen.' Ally would have pressed it but Hope forestalled her. 'Show me what you've got,' she said, making it clear that the subject was closed.

Ally took out her tablet and opened it at the pages she'd shown the princesses, but Hope shook her head. 'Not the diary. It's got the royal seal of approval and I know I can trust you to do a good job. I want to know all about the party on the green.'

Ally talked through her ideas for the 'country fair' party she was planning. The bouquets of cupcakes that would be the centrepieces for the tables in the marquee, buckets of garden flowers, the glorious carousel with its gilded horses.

'It's going to be a family event. I've booked a bouncy castle for the children, I've found a Punch and Judy man and I'm hunting down someone who'll give donkey rides.'

'What fun. I wish we could move the whole damn thing out there and let our hair down.'

'Once the official stuff is over, you'll be able to go out and join in.' She closed her tablet on the pictures of the gilded horses of the carousel. 'In fact it will be expected and if Princess Anna thinks it's beneath her I'll play the *noblesse oblige* card and drag her out there, too.'

Hope laughed, shook her head. 'She's met her match in you.'

'You catch more flies with honey than vinegar. I've been practising my curtsey and I'm being unbelievably respectful. I'm not sure the Dowager is taken in but Anna thinks I'm tame.' Ally glanced at her watch and yelped. 'I have to go.'

'Enjoy your lunch.'

'I'll tell you all about it tonight.'

'Tonight?'

'Oh, didn't I say? Flora and I decided that, as royal bridesmaids, it's our duty to take you for a girl's night out. Celina has fixed it with Princess Anna — I didn't ask what she had to sacrifice — so you can tell Jonas that he has the night off. You are going clubbing.'

9

Ally had just put the finishing touches to her make-up, brushed out her hair and, anticipating a breeze down by the harbour, twisted a scarf around it to keep it in place when her phone rang.

'Fredrik?'

'Ally . . . '

'Is this important?' she said. 'Because I'm going to be late for a very important date.'

'I'm sorry . . . '

Yes, well, she'd realized that he was going to be a no-show the minute he'd said her name.

'I've seen this on those cop shows on the TV,' she said. 'Every time the hero gets a hot date someone finds a body.'

'There isn't a body but you're right — there is a crisis.'

'A security chief's life is not his own,'

she said, swallowing down her disappointment. She expected him to be in a hurry to ring off, but he didn't and she said, 'Your mother called me.'

'She asked for your number. I hope it was okay to give it to her.'

'Dominic gave me her number last night but I didn't want to call her without clearing it with you. She asked if I'd go and see her.'

'What did you say?'

'That I wasn't sure what the palace had arranged. That I would call her.'

'After you'd cleared it with me.'

'Can you bear it?'

'Can you? It's a big step, meeting a guy's mother.'

She heard someone call him. He told them he'd be right there, but instead of saying a hurried goodbye and hanging up he said, 'I managed to get a table at a restaurant with a three-month waiting list. It would be a pity to waste it. I'll send a car and you can pick her up and have lunch together on me.' Again he didn't end the call.

'Hot date?' he queried.

'A figure of speech.'

'Of course. Have you any plans for this evening?'

'Actually, Flora, Hope and I do have something planned.' Was it wrong to feel just a bit glad that she wasn't available? That having dumped her and landed her with his mother he was going to have to work a little bit harder for that hot date.

About to tell him they were going clubbing she stopped herself. Hope wasn't yet a 'face' in San Michele. All that would change after the engagement announcement at the ball, but tonight she would be anonymous, free to be herself. The last thing they needed was a security tail.

'It's a girl's night. You know — pizza, a soppy movie, ice cream.'

'If that's what you consider a good time . . . ' There was another call and he said, 'I have to go.'

'Take care, Fredrik.'

'You too. High heels and cobbles

don't mix. And when you've had enough ice cream, don't call a cab, call me.'

What? He knew! She shook her head. Of course he knew.

'Wait!' She swallowed. 'If there are going be heavies keeping an eye on us, ask them to be discreet. Hope needs a night off from all this.'

'You won't know they're there.'

★   ★   ★

Fredrik was as good as his word.

She'd looked around when they had first arrived but, seeing no obvious surveillance had relaxed and soon forgotten about it as the three of them swigged exotic cocktails, dancing the night away just like they had when they'd all lived in London.

There had been only one brief moment when the crowd had parted and she'd seen Fredrik, uncharacteristically casual in a T-shirt and jeans, leaning against the bar. Their eyes had met for a heart-jolting second before the crowd closed. She hadn't seen him again but she'd known he was there and when, giggling, they had spilled out into the street in the early hours he was waiting.

Flora and Hope piled into the back seat, oblivious to who was holding open the door of the 'cab' she'd ordered, but Fredrik's eyes had met hers through the rear-view mirror and he'd been grinning.

When he'd dropped them off, she'd waved Hope and Flora inside saying that she would sort it.

'Did you have a good time?'

'You were there. What do you think?'

He just smiled, took her hand and walked her to her door.

She opened it, stepped back but he didn't follow. 'I'm on duty.'

'So this is just work?'

'Someone had to keep an eye on our nearly princess letting her hair down.'

'It was just you?' she asked. 'No cocktails, no dancing, no one to talk to.

Just a room full of scantily dressed women dancing their socks off.'

'I didn't notice any socks. Or women.' He reached out and cradled her cheek. 'I only had eyes for you.'

Which was when she grabbed him by his T-shirt, hauled him into her room and threw herself at him.

He caught her, one hand tangling in her hair, one on her rear drawing her into his body so that she could feel his need, exult in it as his mouth claimed hers in the kind of kiss that followed a seven-year drought. A deep, intense, no-holds-barred kiss that was only brought to an end by the need for oxygen.

'I thought you were on duty,' she said, breathlessly.

'My duty was to see you all safely home. Hope is in the hands of her maid; Flora has Max to take care of her. That just leaves you.'

Ally giggled. 'You're going to put me to bed?'

'Do you have any problems with that?'

'Just one.' She gave a little wiggle. 'I'm wearing too many clothes . . . '

His eyes blazing with intention, he deftly unzipped her dress and leaving it in a crumpled heap on the floor, picked her up and carried her to the bed.

She was impatient to see him, touch him. She had her hands full of warm, male-scented T-shirt when his phone rang.

Noooooo!

Her scream of frustration was silent. She had no idea what he said. Her French was good, her Italian passable, but there was a local dialect that he made good use of as he dug his phone out of his back pocket and snapped 'Jensson'.

He listened, ended the call.

The only word she understood was 'Nico' but she could make a good guess at the word he'd used to describe him.

'Don't tell me,' she said. 'You're back on duty.'

'I'm always on damn duty.' He lowered his head so that his forehead touched hers. 'I have to go.'

'Of course you do.'

She held his T-shirt to her face for a moment, breathing in the scent before, with a sigh, she let it fall over his taut stomach.

'It'll calm down after the ball,' he said, holding her for a moment, his kiss a promise that this was only a postponement.

'Just make sure you turn up for that, Prince Charming, or I'll have my fairy godmother turn you into a frog.'

There was another long kiss before, with a groan of frustration, he tore himself away.

★   ★   ★

Ally woke to a thumping head and a dry mouth but it had been worth it. It had been a great night. Not perfect. In a perfect world Fredrik would not have been dragged away to deal with Nico's drama but it had been wonderful to see Hope letting her hair down and having fun.

She eased herself out of bed, downed a glass of water and a couple of painkillers and checked her texts. The only one that she was interested in was one from Fredrik. Just one word. 'Tonight.'

She shook her head. Barring some crisis . . . Then she smiled. There were places in Combe St Philip, quiet dells in the woods where the grass was soft and there was no phone signal.

She was trying to talk herself into getting up and going for a run when her phone beeped. Fredrik . . .

She grabbed her phone, grinning as she opened the text. It wasn't from Fredrik; it was from Flora.

Hope and Jonas had done a bunk.

*   *   *

Instead of Fizzing with anticipation at the prospect of the gala ball, the promise implicit in Fredrik's text, Ally spent the day worrying about Hope.

The night out, letting her hair down, was supposed to shake out the tension,

196

but clearly it had done the opposite and given a focus to her doubts.

She'd sent a message to Max letting him know that she was with Jonas, that they just needed thinking time away from the palace. They'd left it very late but you couldn't argue with the think twice, marry once approach.

Ally doubted that Princess Anna would be terribly upset if the engagement didn't happen but the ball was officially to celebrate Jonas's birthday. If the major player didn't show she was going to be madder than a wet hen and looking to someone to blame.

There were three candidates.

Fredrik, for allowing Hope to escape the palace — although Jonas, having lived there as a boy, must surely know a dozen ways to avoid security.

Nico, for whatever he'd done to cause a diversion. Neither of them were in evidence this morning to ask.

And finally, there was her. If Anna discovered how assiduously Fredrik had taken his duty to 'see her home' safely,

Ally knew she was going to be in very hot water.

Celina had taken Flora and Max and the children to some beauty spot for the day. She had a full day meeting the palace PR team, getting their 'quotes' for the diary, taking photographs. Trying not to check her phone every ten minutes hoping for news.

Meanwhile there was no drama, no alarm in the palace. Anna asked her if she'd seen Hope and she could answer honestly that she had not. The Dowager had suggested that she might have gone with Hope and Max, or be spending the day with Jonas.

Anna hadn't exactly sniffed, but she shrugged, tactfully agreed with her mother-in-law — who would dare do otherwise — that it would be good for Hope to have a relaxing day away from the palace and left it at that.

If Fredrik had known, he would undoubtedly have been at her door demanding to know what she knew. She wouldn't have lied to him; she wouldn't have had to. She had no idea where they were.

She'd been torn about whether to call him, warn him, but Hope was, always would be, her very best friend and if she needed time, then she must have it. The world wouldn't come to an end if there was no announcement tonight. Probably.

She called Flora but she must have been out of range because it just went to voice mail. When they returned there was still no news and there was nothing to do but cross their fingers and get ready for the ball.

Shower, hair, nails, make-up. She was used to getting ready in minutes but she took everything slowly, concentrating on each detail; she didn't want to be standing around, fretting, waiting for the footman to escort her to the ballroom.

She checked her cell for texts, hoping for something.

Fredrik's text mocked her.

Tonight?

It seemed unlikely that was going to

happen but she stepped into her underwear. She hadn't been able to afford a new dress but she'd indulged in some just-in-case matching lace undies. Just in case the frisson of awareness between her and Fredrik had developed into something more tangible.

It had, but if Hope and Jonas didn't turn up tonight they'd all be on the next plane home.

Cattle class.

Her dress was a weighty, rich burgundy silk, made for her by a local dressmaker who'd added a few useful extras. You didn't get seam pockets in designer dresses.

Simple, figure skimming, the kind of classic style that never went out of date. Shoes. A pair of gold and ruby earrings that she'd been given for her eighteenth birthday. Her grandmother's gold locket. Gold elbow-length fingerless lace gloves.

She had just slipped her phone into its special little seam pocket — shaped so that it wouldn't slip out — lippie and tissues into her clutch bag when there was a tap at the door.

It was a man in uniform but it wasn't a footman.

She caught her breath. 'Fredrik . . . '

He was wearing dress blues with enough gold braid to gladden a haberdasher's heart. Over it he wore a scarlet sash on which was pinned a gold and enamel order. He looked positively edible and she thought she might just swoon with lust.

'I'm giving you fair warning,' she said. 'If anyone wants you to deal with some idiot climbing the palace wall tonight, they are going to have to come through me.'

'My deputy is in charge of security tonight. I'm unavailable for anything short of World War Three.' He offered her his arm. 'Shall we go?'

She slipped her hand beneath his arm. 'Fredrik, on the subject of World War Three — '

'You look beautiful, Ally.'

The compliment was so unexpected that she blushed. *Blushed!* Like a fifteen-year-old, but before she could stammer out a thank you, he apparently changed his mind.

'No . . . ' *What* . . . ? 'You don't need make-up, a fabulous dress for that. You were beautiful that first morning, without a scrap of make-up, in a pinafore that looked as if it had been worn by your grandmother. Tonight you'd make Cinderella weep with envy.' He stopped, glanced down. 'Are you wearing glass slippers?'

He'd remembered what she'd told him that first morning, she realized. About taking it in turns with Hope to wear the Cinderella dress. That was better than any compliment.

'Not glass — ' she lifted her skirt a little to show him red shoes that matched her dress ' — I always thought glass would be desperately dangerous. And uncomfortable.' She looked up. 'Will you still be my Prince Charming?'

'Ask me again when the clock strikes midnight,' he said, heading towards the ballroom.

'I have to wait that long?'

He didn't blush but he stumbled and beneath the high collar of his jacket she saw him swallow.

'I hope that's not your dancing leg.'

'Ally . . . ' He paused, took a breath. 'I'm fine. Have you had a useful day?' he asked. 'I understand you've been dashing all over place, buttonholing anyone who would talk to you.'

'Everyone has been very helpful. Fredrik . . . ' She couldn't let him walk into this blind, but just as she was about to blurt out what had happened, his phone rang. 'Off duty?' she demanded.

He kept walking as he checked the caller ID before accepting the call.

'Jensson.' He said nothing else, just listened, then switched the phone off before sliding it into his pocket. 'Now I'm off duty, unlike you. As a royal bridesmaid and PR person, I think you're supposed to be smiling.'

They had reached the foot of the impressive, sweeping flight of steps that led up to the ballroom. For one crazy moment she considered staging a fall to provide a distraction. Fredrik would have to take her to the emergency room and they'd both be out of the firing line when Princess Anna realized that her evening was about to be a disaster.

Tempting as it was, she couldn't leave Flora and Max to face it alone so she took a breath, jacked her face up into her professional smile and negotiated the steps without tripping over her hem. Ignoring the gilded swags, the glitter of chandeliers, the men in uniform, the fabulous dresses, she sought out Flora, caught her eye and got an imperceptible shake of the head.

Unlike the reception, the last thing she wanted was a clear head and she took the glass of champagne that Fredrik handed her and drank it down in one go.

'Are you all right, Ally?' Fredrik asked as she snagged another glass from a passing waiter. 'You seem a little tense.'

Tense? She felt as if she was about to

crack but before she could tell him why, there was a rustle of frocks, a sudden silence and as she turned she saw Jonas and Hope standing in the doorway. Hope looked radiant, Jonas jubilant as he introduced his fiancee to the assembled guests.

The second glass of champagne followed the first.

'Better now?' Fredrik said, taking the glass and parking it on a passing tray.

She looked up at him. 'You knew, didn't you?' He wasn't exactly smiling but there was that telltale crease at the corner of his mouth. 'You knew all the time. That was Jonas just now, wasn't it? Calling you to let you know he was on his way.'

He shrugged. 'Hope texted Max to reassure him. Jonas texted me in case Anna decided to call out the troops.'

'To do what?' He didn't answer. 'Drag them back? Were you supposed to make her back off? I'm not sure there's a medal big enough for that one.'

'Jonas and I are friends, Ally. We sat

205

in the same classrooms, played on the same teams, covered for one another. Found ways in and out of the palace that no one else knew about. He was there when I was brought home more dead than alive. When being alive seemed like the bad option.'

Jonas, she thought, was his Hope, and her relief that the runaways had returned in time to save the show was washed away in a rush of regret that she hadn't called him this morning.

'I'm sorry,' she said. 'I should have called you as soon as I knew they were gone. I wanted to tell you . . . I was trying to tell you just now.'

'A bit late, Ally.'

'So you thought you'd let me sweat?'

The promise of a smile had gone and a muscle worked in his jaw as he said, 'I wanted you to trust me.'

She swallowed. She was protesting too much and he didn't believe her. Not quite. She'd chosen friendship over the possibility of whatever 'tonight' might have led to.

'It's your job, Fredrik,' she said, turning away to applaud as a slow waltz began to play and Jonas took Hope in his arms to dance her around the ballroom; to hide the fact that for some reason her eyes appeared to be watering. 'You told me yourself, you are never off duty.'

'That's something I need to change.' After a few moments, other people began to join in and Fredrik said, 'I think this dance is slow enough for a crock like me. Unless you'd rather wait for someone else?'

She didn't want to dance. She wanted to run away and hide somewhere, but like Fredrik she was on duty so she jacked up her smile. 'My mother, or possibly my grandmother, taught me that the first dance should always be with the man or woman you arrived with,' she said, turning to him. 'After that you can go and put your feet . . .'

The words died on her lips as he touched a crooked finger to her lower lid. 'Is that a tear?'

'It might be,' she admitted as it spilt over and soaked into his glove. 'I cry at soppy movies, too. And puppies on Facebook. I have even been known to get emotional at the first sighting of baby ducks.'

'Who are you?' he asked. 'What have you done with Ally Parker, hard-nosed gossip writer?'

'It's true,' she said. 'Ask Flora. She'll tell you that I have to use industrial-strength waterproof mascara.' Unable to hold his gaze, she looked across at Jonas and Hope. 'I was worried about Hope — we both were — but it's obvious that whatever was wrong, Jonas has fixed it.'

'You and he have a great deal in common.'

She swallowed, shook her head. 'Too heavy. This is a party, Fredrik. Let's dance.'

He looked at her for a moment longer, but then his hand was at her waist, her hand in his. He was from that class where boys were taught to dance and he guided her slowly around the ballroom until, as the floor became more crowded, he drew her closer and she wasn't aware of moving at all. Only of her cheek against Fredrik's jacket, his arm around her. Of breathing in the scent of clean linen, soap, warm skin and never wanting this moment to stop.

Too soon the set ended and the orchestra struck up something livelier. Prince Nico claimed a dance and Fredrik surrendered her. 'Time to do your duty, Cinderella. Just make sure that tonight, when the clock strikes twelve, we have a date.'

She rested a hand briefly on his arm, held his gaze for a moment. 'You'll find my shoe on the stair,' she promised.

* * *

Fredrik watched as Nico twirled her away to dance to something fast but she moved on before the music slowed again, waltzing with old courtiers, quickstepping with royal cousins and dancing something very silly with Prince Carlo but when she turned her eyes always found him.

Jonas joined him for a moment, not saying anything as he followed his gaze, watching as Ally produced a mobile phone from some hidden pocket to take a selfie with Carlo.

'How does she get away with that?' he asked. 'Anna expressively forbade phones. More to the point why are you over here watching her when you could be dancing?'

'She's somehow managed to convince Anna that she's housebroken. I believe it has something to do with the quality of her curtsey.'

'That would do it.'

'As for the rest, it's not who you dance with, Jonas. It's who you leave with.'

Jonas briefly touched his arm, a gesture that encompassed a lifetime of friendship.

Ten minutes later the supper gong sounded and Ally was at his side.

'Having a good time?' he asked as she leaned against him, a little flushed from dancing and too much champagne.

She groaned. 'I've smiled so much that my face feels as if it's about to crack in half and much as I hate to admit it, I danced myself to a standstill last night.' She looked up. 'Please tell me it's twelve o'clock.'

'Not even close,' he said, 'but I imagine Prince Charming, if he had anything about him, would have invited Cinderella to take a reviving breath of air in his rose garden.'

'Lucky Cinderella,' she said, fanning herself with her hand.

'It's too early for roses but would stars make an adequate substitute?'

'Stars . . . '

She stopped fanning herself and as she looked up they were both remembering that moment in Combe St Philip when he'd told her about the stars in the mountains.

'The air will be seriously fresh,' he warned. 'You might want to change into something warmer.'

'Warmer?'

'Tank, T-shirt, shirt, sweater. I'll be waiting in the courtyard.'

Without another word they broke away from the crowd moving towards the buffet supper.

'This feels so naughty,' she said as they reached the grand staircase. 'Like leaving a party without saying thank you to your hostess.'

'I'll send her flowers,' he said.

'Everyone will send her flowers. Surprise her. Send her chocolates.'

'Chocolates?'

'I'll bet no one ever sends her chocolates.'

'Does she look like a woman who eats chocolate?'

'She looks like a woman who should have temptation put in her way.'

10

As Ally crossed the vast lobby she was doing a good impression of a swan. On the surface everything was serene, graceful as she calmly smiled her thanks to the footman who leapt to open a door for her. Underneath everything was in turmoil.

Her heart and pulse were racing each other as if they were competing in a hundred-yard sprint. Her stomach was churning with excitement, nerves, a whole load of emotions that she couldn't pin down.

Once she was out of sight of the flunkies, Ally took off her shoes and ran. By the time she reached her door her dress was unzipped and five minutes later she was wrapped up in her warmest clothes.

She had no idea how far they would have to go to leave the lights of the city behind but it was unlikely she'd get a signal so the last thing she did was open her tablet and despatch the emails she'd drafted to her mother and the vicar. Then, as an afterthought, she flicked through the photographs she snapped that night and sent the one of her and Prince Carlo as an attachment to her mother. Because she deserved it.

She tossed it, along with her phone, into the big shoulder bag in which she carried everything she might need, ever, and hurried out to the courtyard.

Fredrik flashed the lights of a big 4x4 to attract her attention, then leaned across to push the door open.

He looked her over as she settled in her seat, raising his eyebrows when he reached her boots. 'You came prepared.'

'There's nothing in the diary for tomorrow so I was going to ask the palace press office if they could arrange a trip into the mountains.'

'Why?'

'Because they're there?' she offered.

'And the real reason?'

Because they were his place, had been his life and she wanted to feel something of what he felt when he was high up, breathing thin air, risking his life. Because she wanted to know him better.

'I'm going to write about San Michele on my 'royal bridesmaid' blog,' she said. Also true.

'What bridesmaid blog?' Before she could answer he said, 'Don't answer that. I don't want to know.'

'The press office are totally happy with it,' she said, taking no notice. 'So is Princess Anna. San Michele is making a huge effort to attract tourists, film crews, anyone who will bring money into the country.'

'I had heard,' he said, less than enthusiastically. 'They are all spitting pips that the wedding won't be held here.'

'A wedding isn't a promo opportunity but their frustration is understandable so I'm doing my bit to maximize exposure. They are very excited about the possibility that one of the gossip magazines might do a feature on the country.'

'Is there anyone in San Michele you haven't managed to charm?' he asked.

'You?' she suggested.

That seemed to throw him and for once he had no comeback.

'Admit it, Fredrik, you fancy me, you're up for a fling, but I don't for a minute believe that you're charmed by me.'

She thought, hoped that he was going to deny it. Instead he slammed the 4x4 into gear and headed out of the palace grounds.

She'd spoken the truth and his response was honest, if not quite what she'd been hoping for but this, whatever this was, would not survive beyond the wedding and it was far better that deep emotions were not engaged.

Even as she thought it she knew she was kidding herself. Her emotions had been engaged from the first moment she'd seen him. They had been a very mixed assortment, to be true, but tangled up with the irritation, amusement, a very strong impulse to be naked with him, there was something deeper that was entirely new. A feeling that she did not recognize, but suspected that when it was all over, was going to leave her feeling empty.

Fredrik seemed disinclined to talk and Ally settled herself back in her seat, looking around as they climbed out beyond the city, passing first through farmland, then plunging into thick forest where the only light was from their headlights.

They turned off the main road and drove down a forest road for a while until, without warning, they were back in the open on a track crossing high alpine pasture.

An owl, drifting low over the ground, was caught in their headlights but as she turned to Fredrik to ask if there were wolves in the mountains, or bears, she could see that his jaw had noticeably tensed.

'Fredrik . . . '

Climbing was Fredrik's passion. Like his father before him.

His mother had spilled it all out over lunch. His father had been warned of the danger but being on the mountains mattered more to him than life or death. If he was going to die he didn't want to be strapped to a hospital monitor but high up on a rock face.

'Fredrik was climbing with his father almost as soon as he could walk. He was fourteen when I married Alessandro. He refused to come to the wedding, instead climbing San Michele's highest peak solo to plant his father's flag on the summit.' She sighed. 'He hasn't been near the mountains since his injury. It has been a far greater loss than Eloise.'

'Ally?'

Fredrik glanced across at her. She'd been going to say that they didn't have to go any further. They were high enough. The only visible lights were far below where fishing villages were strung out along the coast.

'Shall I put on some music?' she suggested.

He shrugged and she sorted through CDs stacked in the storage box between them.

There was an eclectic mix. Rock, jazz, classic. An Elgar Cello Concerto recorded by Eloise Jakolin.

She put it back, grabbed something else but before she could stuff it into the player, he reached out, caught her hand to stop her. 'Play it.' He didn't wait for her, flipped the case open, pushed the CD home and drove on as the slow opening to the concerto covered the silence.

What had started out as an exciting adventure had gone downhill from the moment she'd got in the car. Ten minutes later he pulled over, turned off the engine, but he didn't move, didn't speak until, what seemed like hours later, the music stopped.

'Did Dominic tell you about Eloise?' he asked.

She shook her head. 'Your mother.'

She turned in her seat to face him, not prepared to sit there feeling guilty for having raked up something he would rather forget. 'Isn't that why you wanted me to have lunch with her? So that she could talk about you. Tell me the things you find it hard to talk about?'

The fact that he'd met Eloise Jakolin at university, fallen in love with her, that she'd won some international music prize and while Fredrik was struggling to walk, she was busy booking international tours . . .

'It doesn't matter,' she said.

No man reached his thirties without having some kind of relationship. She'd been in one herself but nothing serious enough to survive the move home to Combe St Philip. The lack of support when she'd needed it had stung but Nick had made no bones about the fact that he wasn't the kind of man to waste his weekends hanging out in a country village.

It was nothing compared to Fredrik's

loss of both his passion and his love.

'I've already told you more than anyone else, Ally. I would have told you about Eloise if it had been important. My mother wanted to meet you.'

'Why?'

Good question, Fredrik thought.

His mother had obviously heard something that made her think that this was a lot more than a fling, no doubt from the Dowager who could read a man's thoughts before he was thinking them.

He didn't say that. Instead he opened the door, walked across the meadow, looking up at the dark shapes of the mountains. The memory of the rock beneath his fingers, the feel of his toes clinging to tiny clefts, the sharp, thin air was so strong that for a moment he felt dizzy.

He reached out, without thinking, for support and Ally was there beside him, her breath misty in the icy air and, without a word, he lifted an arm and drew her close.

'Eloise flew back from America when I was injured.' He could still see her face, the mix of concern and dread easy to read when you knew someone as well as he'd known her. 'She wanted to wait for me to recover and I have no doubt that when she said it, she meant it.'

'How long?'

'The doctors said six months. Maybe more. A lifetime when you're building a career as a solo artist.'

Ally felt something in her crack as she recognized the emotion that had been eluding her for what it was and she shivered, but not with cold.

'You loved her so much that you sent her away.'

'You flatter me, Ally. While she was playing here in San Michele, a soloist with the national orchestra, we had a future, but the moment she won that competition and international stardom beckoned, I knew it was over.'

Ally had once asked Laura Chase how she had been able to walk away from a career as a concert pianist to become the wife of a young curate. She'd said that it had been the easiest decision of her life.

Fredrik had loved Eloise enough to send her away. That she'd gone suggested that he had been right but he must have hoped . . .

She leaned into him, a gesture of comfort and his arm tightened around her. 'I was mobile a lot sooner than anyone had thought possible and I could have followed her but a man has to have a purpose, Ally. I'm not made to be a coat carrier, to trail in the wake of someone else's glory.'

'That's painfully honest.'

'Which is why I hope you'll believe me when I say that knowing she's happy, fulfilled, being the person she wants to be means that I can listen to her play with pleasure rather than regret.'

He had opened the door for the woman he'd loved and she'd walked through it.

'That's what you do, isn't it?' she said, a lump the size of a golf ball in her throat. 'You protect the people you love. You protected your mother; you protected your brother and sister from what you believed to be the truth. You protected Eloise from having to stay and nurse you. You give and give and give . . .'

She looked up at the dark shape of the mountains against the blazing sky, star-shine picking out a glimmer of white at their peaks, in the hollows where the sun had not reached.

'You're doing it now. Dominic told me that you haven't been back to the mountains since you were injured and yet you've brought me here so that I can see the stars.'

'I had a different mountain to climb.' He looked down at her. 'I'm here today because I wanted to give you something big enough, important enough to show my gratitude for what you've done for me and my family.'

She opened her mouth to tell him that she didn't want his gratitude but he touched a finger to her lips.

'I'm here for me, too.' He lifted his

hand, curved it around her cold cheek and, when she continued to look up at him, he lowered his mouth to hers.

It wasn't the crazy, rip-your-clothes-off kind of kiss that had taken them tumbling onto the four-poster bed in her room. His touch was tentative and then he drew back a little, giving her a moment to consider if this was what she wanted because suddenly the stakes were much higher than sex.

Her own lips trembled a little and then, as she whispered his name, a whimpering plea for more, he grasped her hand and headed back to the 4x4.

That was it? They were leaving?

He opened the door, grabbed the bag she'd brought with her and a backpack from the back seat and, her hand still grasped tightly in his, he headed into the dark.

'Wait! I can't see where I'm going,' she said, stumbling after him, crashing into him as he stopped without warning. There was the scrape of a stone and then the sound of a key being turned in a lock.

There was a hut? Somewhere for climbers to rest, stay overnight?

She had no idea what to expect. Something very basic with bunks she suspected, but when Fredrik struck a match, lit a lamp and hung it over a table, in the shadows she saw pine walls, a stone fireplace with a wood-burning stove with an oven, an updated version of the sort of thing she'd seen in a Victorian house run by the National Trust. There were a couple of armchairs and a rug and, as the lamp steadied, grew brighter, she realized that there was a kitchen corner with cupboards, a small sink, a gas burner. And, in an alcove, there was a three-quarter-size bed.

Fredrik lit the stove, filled a kettle at a small sink and set it on the stove.

'Running water?'

'There's a spring. It's piped in and when I pull the plug it goes into a filtration pit. It's going to take a while to heat through,' he said.

The hut or the kettle? It didn't matter, she wasn't waiting another minute for this man.

'In that case,' she said, 'we'll have to think of some other way to keep warm.'

'Ally . . . '

She didn't want him to ask her if she was sure. To tell her that this wasn't a relationship that could go anywhere. She wanted him, hot and vital inside her, and she wanted him now and it was her turn to put her fingers over his mouth . . . It was only when she was certain of his silence that she reached up and unwound the scarf from his neck and tossed it onto a chair.

Then she took hold of his jacket zip, hauled it down and when it was open she slid her hands inside the layers of clothes he was wearing and warmed them against his skin.

After that she couldn't have said who did what except that she slipped the button of his jeans and Fredrik's hungry kiss was burning her up, making the fire redundant. And then her hands were inside his pants, cradling his backside as he lifted her against him so that she could feel the strength of his need. Then it was her name on Fredrik's lips as she pushed them down, her hands stroking the backs of long sinewy legs, sliding over the ridges of scar tissue, as she sank to her knees.

She'd never done that before, left herself completely open, defenceless, with any man but if he had changed, so had she. She'd faced her demons and was stronger, no longer guarding herself. For the first time she was able to give herself fully, freely. Or maybe Fredrik was the first man who'd inspired such trust.

His groan of pleasure filled her with a sense of her own power and when he pushed his fingers through her hair, lifted her to her feet and responded with a searing kiss, she knew she was lost.

Later, lying back in Fredrik's arms beneath a down comforter, with only the flicker of the firelight dancing around the walls, Ally said, 'This is where you were today.'

'What makes you say that?'

'Everything was clean, the fire laid, the bed aired, protection within reach.'

'This morning there was a genuine emergency but yes, I came up here this afternoon to lay some ghosts, clear out the cobwebs.'

She could have handled a few cobwebs but the ones he was referring to were the metaphorical kind. He'd faced up to the loss of who he was and this, whatever this was, was an interlude, a pause while he gathered himself.

'Are you hungry?' he asked.

'I'm absolutely starving,' she said, straddling him. 'Feed me.'

★   ★   ★

It was nearly dawn when Fredrik cooked bacon and eggs on top of the stove. Ally made coffee and they took it outside to watch as the sky turned silver, then bubbles of cloud turned pink and the sun rose, flooding the valley far below them with golden light.

'Have you got any interviews lined up for today?' he asked, when they were clearing up breakfast. Washing dishes as if they were a couple.

'Nothing. The only thing on my agenda today was to persuade someone to bring me up here.'

'Job done, then. You'll find a new toothbrush in the shower.'

'Totally prepared,' she said. 'You only have to arrive somewhere without your luggage once to discover the advisability of tucking a spare toothbrush and set of underwear in your handbag.' She dried the last fork, hung up the cloth near the fire to dry and said, 'So, do you want to show me how the shower works?'

The shower was fun, the sex hot. Afterwards, wearing all the spare layers they could find, they walked up the mountain until they reached a pocket of snow where they built a snowman, made snow angels and, like a couple of kids, laughed as they had a snowball fight. They returned wet and frozen to the hut and fell shivering into bed, to warm one another.

'Do you want to go back tonight?' he asked later.

'No ... ' The word slipped out, leaving her no hiding place, but she was pretty sure she could stay there forever. Not going to happen. 'But Flora will be wondering where I am,' she said. 'And we leave tomorrow morning.'

'Send her a text. Ask her to pack for you. I'll get you there on time.'

Another night with Fredrik?

'You have a signal?'

'This is the highest place where a helicopter can land,' he said. 'The hut is used by the mountain rescue team and they installed a communications beacon.'

'Of course. You can't ever be out of touch.'

'I haven't turned my phone on,' he assured her.

'Nor me.' No doubt there would be texts, missed calls, from her mother, the vicar, quite possibly the editor of

Celebrity but she wasn't letting the world into this magic place. This magic moment. 'I'll text her later.'

'I'll stick some potatoes in to cook, then.'

When it was dark, Fredrik helped her set up her camera with a long exposure to capture the sky while they spent a quiet evening in front of the fire finishing up the bottle of red wine that Fredrik had opened to go with the steaks he'd cooked.

They talked, laughed, made love and overslept.

That was good. It meant that in the rush to get back to Liburno and make her plane, there was no time for long, difficult goodbyes with promises that in the light of day might be regretted. She frantically texted Flora, asking her to pack her things and Fredrik arrived on the apron of the airfield with minutes to spare.

No time for a kiss, just a mad scramble from the 4x4 to the aircraft steps before they were pulled away. By

the time she flopped into a seat —
mouthing a silent 'tell you later' to
Flora — and turned to wave, Fredrik
was driving away.

★ ★ ★

Once she was home, Ally had little
chance to daydream about the time
spent with Fredrik on the mountain.

Her mother had asked if she'd seen
him. She hadn't denied it, but explained
that he was palace security and the 'kiss'
that had been all around the village had
been no more than a ruse to conceal the
real reason for his visit to Combe St
Philip. Which was true.

An agent she knew and trusted had
taken on the wedding diary, dealing with
publishers, negotiating pre-wedding magazine excerpts and foreign rights, earning
her fifteen per cent ten times over.

A temporary cover, a sweet picture of
a much younger Hope with her beloved
pony, was already online and pre-sales
figures were ridiculous.

Everyone was pitching in to help with the Wedding on the Green, the WI ladies were practising their cupcake posies, flowers had been pledged, a giant screen booked so that everyone could see the wedding. She still had to come up with a way to keep out uninvited guests. Including the press.

Max had already tossed out half a dozen photographers creeping around the grounds of Hasebury Hall and, as anticipated, villagers had been offered cash for scandal. They had, against all odds, closed ranks and, after a number of 'incidents', there was a permanent police presence in the village; but she worried about security on the day.

Not for the wedding — that was Fredrik's job — but for the village green party.

She asked him if he had any ideas and they had exchanged a number of totally businesslike emails that had no reason to make her heart leap whenever one dropped into her inbox. He asked questions about where this was, where that could go and she had replied.

It was, as she'd told Flora and Hope, a holiday fling. They lived a thousand miles apart. End of.

It wasn't even as if they would have to spend much time together at the wedding. They might, for tidiness, be a couple but he would be focused on security while she would be fully occupied doing her bridesmaid thing in church and immediately the service was over she would be looking at the photographs, choosing which ones would go on the jacket and getting them to the publisher's assistant waiting at the printer so that the wedding diary would be printed and piled high in bookshops and the supermarkets the next day.

At least that was what she kept telling herself but the reality confronted her every time she opened her laptop or tablet and saw the long exposure photograph she'd taken of the stars. Saw how far the world had turned while they'd sat in front of the fire, gazing into the flames, words unnecessary. While they'd sat beneath a blazing sky and watched for shooting stars. While they'd made love.

But she didn't have time to mourn a relationship that never had a chance. She'd delegated a lot of the Wedding on the Green organization to her mother, but she was still working two jobs, putting together the wedding diary, writing her blog as well as dashing into London for dress fittings and publisher meetings after her lunchtime stint at the Old Forge.

Penny had taken on an extra member of staff to deal with increased numbers of visitors coming to the village, but it was still a scrum to get a table most days and when the bell rang to announce another arrival she gave a silent groan. If one more person asked her if they could take a selfie with her, she might just scream.

But she forced a smile, turned to explain that it would be half an hour before a table was free and found herself looking at Fredrik.

His appearance was so unexpected that it was if as the clock had been turned back to that morning in the Three Bells.

The overcoat had been replaced by a dark grey suit, but the white shirt, a silk tie banded in the dark red and gold colours of San Michele were the same. And his eyes, the slate grey of a threatening sky, his intense gaze, had the same bone-melting quality.

The only difference was that the heart-stopping breath-seizing response was multiplied tenfold because now she knew what it was like to lose herself to his touch, wake up in his arms, light up to the smile he kept under lock and key.

Last time she'd gone to him to put on a show for Jennifer Harmon. This time it was real and her feet were glued to the floor.

11

Ally had no idea how long she stood there before Penny said, 'We haven't got a table at the moment, sir. If you could come back in half an hour we could squeeze you in.'

'No need. I was just hoping for a word with Ally. If you can spare her for a moment?'

The sexy, barely there accent gave him away and Penny turned to her, eyes wide as she mouthed, 'He's the kiss man?'

She swallowed, managed what she hoped was a careless shrug.

'Off you go,' she said, waving her away with a grin. 'We can manage here.'

About to protest, Ally, realizing that she was now the focus of several dozen pairs of eyes, whipped off her apron, grabbed her bag, and held up a 'do not say a word' hand as Fredrik held the door for her. She stepped out into the street.

'The kiss man?'

She groaned. 'You can lip-read.'

'Oh, I think everyone in the room got that message.' It would have been okay if he'd smiled, but he was back to his poker face and she was getting nothing . . .

'I made it absolutely clear, when I came back from San Michele, that you only kissed me to cover up your real reason for being in Combe St Philip.'

'Did they believe you?'

She shook her head. 'Not for a minute.'

'Good,' he said, and then he kissed her, right there in the street with the entire café watching and, just like that first time, she kissed him right back.

A youth speeding by on a bike, rang his bell and whistled encouragement.

'We have to stop meeting like this . . . ' Ally's voice was shaking as Fredrik drew back, but then so were her knees and just about every other part of her.

'Why?' He took her arm and headed down the street. 'It works for me.'

'Does it?' He frowned. 'I didn't know . . . I wasn't sure . . . ' She pulled herself together. 'You are a lousy correspondent.'

'You wanted love letters?'

'I want nothing . . . ' That was so not true . . . 'Perhaps a little more than a dear sir, yours sincerely email.'

'Never put in an email something you wouldn't want the whole world to read.'

Like what? 'Hello, how are you? would have done.'

'No, Ally, it wouldn't.'

No . . . 'You could have phoned.'

'Really? Phone sex?'

'Is that all we have? Sex?' She stopped. Of course it was. 'Fredrik, we both know this isn't going anywhere.'

'It's a little soon to be thinking about a destination. Let's just concentrate on the journey for now. Are you free this evening?'

'No. I've got diary pages to put together, a blog to write.'

'So there's no point in asking you out on a date?'

'A date?'

'You've heard of them. Holding hands in the cinema, dinner somewhere quiet?'

'Who are you? And what have you done with Fredrik Jensson?' His only answer was to tuck her hand under his arm and head down the street. 'And where are we going?'

'Your village no-parking rule meant I had to leave my car at the Hall.'

'You're staying there?'

'No, I'm staying in London but I'm on my way to discuss security arrangements for the wedding with the Chief Constable. My appointment is in half an hour, which is why we have to keep walking.'

'One kiss and you're gone?'

'Oh, Ally . . . ' His face softened and for a moment she thought he was going to say something but then he shook his head. 'I'm staying in London for two reasons. One, and this isn't for general consumption, Prince Carlo and Princess Anna are coming to England the week before the wedding to attend a number of social engagements, including a gala performance by Eloise. Security arrangements have to be made with the hotel and the Festival Hall.'

'Oh, right.' Would he see her? Of course he'd see her . . .

History. Eloise was history, she told herself. Fredrik was here with her.

'Two, while I have no doubt that Max would have given me a bed for the night, I'd rather spend what little spare time I have with you. So, unless you'd rather be tucked up with your laptop this evening, I'll pick you up at about four.'

Fredrik was here with her and asking her out on a date. The blog could wait.

'I'll be in my office at the Hall.'

'Shame. I was looking forward to a cup of tea and a slice of your mother's cake. Another time, perhaps.'

'Be careful, Fredrik, I might take you seriously.'

'Anyone who knows me will tell you

that I am a very serious man.'

'Okay, then seriously, let's make it the quiet dinner.'

'Did you have anywhere special in mind?'

Ally had no doubt that he could get a table in anywhere but it wasn't about being seen in a smart restaurant, or even the food, it was about being together.

'Room service?' she suggested.

Fredrik stopped. 'I wasn't . . . ' He made an oddly helpless gesture for a man who was so controlled, so together. 'I just wanted to spend some quality time with you without the constant risk of some emergency calling me away.'

'Me too but without the buckets of popcorn, a rubbish movie, waiters who keep popping by to make sure everything is to our satisfaction. We could always go for a walk afterwards. In one of the parks or along the embankment?'

They never made it along the embankment.

Fredrik's suite at Claridge's had everything they needed for a close encounter. A bed the size of a tennis court, a fabulous bathroom with a bath big enough for two and dinner served by a butler who, having made sure they had everything they needed, made a discreet exit.

It felt, Ally thought, like a brief honeymoon. Absolutely perfect.

★　★　★

'I've been thinking about a hen party.' It was four weeks to the wedding. Ally, Hope and Flora were in London for their final dress fittings and they were celebrating the occasion with supper at their favourite Italian restaurant.

'Oh, no, you're not distracting us that easily,' Hope said. 'We want to hear all about you and Fredrik.'

'There's nothing to tell.'

'Oh, come on. He turned up in Combe St Philip, kissed you in front of dozens of people before whisking you off to London for a *date*. Who does that any more?'

'It's just a fling, ladies — move on, nothing to see.' Ally had stuck firmly to that line after her disappearing act in San Michele, and she wasn't budging just because Flora had seen Fredrik pick her up at the Hall.

'Where did he take you? Fancy restaurant, the theatre, back row of the cinema . . . Come on, you have to give us something!'

'All those were on offer,' she replied, 'and we did have dinner but since time was short, I opted for room service.'

'Whoa! So it was a *hot* date,' Flora said, grinning.

'Hot as Hades since you're asking but Fredrik will leave with the royal party the day after the wedding and, with luck and a following wind, I'll be fighting off job offers. End of.'

'If the gossip mags had any sense they would be lining up,' Hope said.

'They are. Even the man who sacked me has suggested that he might have been a little hasty and invited me down for a 'chat over lunch' to discuss my 'career prospects'.'

'Somewhere expensive I hope,' Flora said.

'Never going to happen.'

'If you've given up on the gossip magazines, what are you going to do?' Hope asked.

'To be honest I've loved doing this PR stuff.'

'You've done an amazing job, giving the media what they need without me having to get involved.'

'Your job is to marry a prince. Mine is to show the world how it happened.'

The diary was down to the last few pages. Dress fittings, hen party, last moments with her friends and family.

Her bridesmaid blog had been featured in all the gossip magazines, the editors no doubt hoping to earn enough brownie points to get a chance of some exclusive photographs, or an interview with the bride.

So far they had all been scooped by the local county magazine, which had run a feature on Sir Max's landscape business; and a glossy cookery magazine had interviewed Flora on her role as royal wedding chef. They had been too polite to push for details of her menu, but there had been a photograph of the jars of San Michele honey lined up on her pantry shelves and a number of local sweet recipes in which it featured.

Since it had appeared Flora had received a number of offers from magazines and publishers and a famous department store had started stocking the honey.

'If a chance to get into PR, serious stuff, came up . . . '

'You should grab the moment, Ally, and start up on your own.'

'Nice thought but no money,' she said, reaching into her bag for her notebook. 'Hen party?' she reminded them. 'I thought the Friday before the wedding — '

'Hold on,' Flora said. 'We're getting away from the important stuff here.'

'What can be more important than

Hope's hen party?'

They both looked at her as if she was mad. 'Fredrik?'

'Jonas said he's seemed like a different man since you came to San Michele,' Hope said, with that upward inflection that invited a confidence.

'He's been reunited with his family,' Ally pointed out.

He'd faced his mountain — both real and metaphorical — and although their lives would separate after the wedding, she knew he would never forget her, just as she would never forget him.

'But — '

But . . .

There had been a second weekend, nearer to home in a country hotel near Bath, and while she was still getting those curt businesslike emails from Fredrik, the post brought postcards, discreetly tucked into envelopes, to her office at the Hall. Pictures of his mountains, the harbour at San Michele, views of the castle, a crystal clear mountain lake. And on the reverse always the same four words. Sometimes with a question mark. Sometimes without.

Wish you were here.

She swallowed down the lump that rose in her throat.

'But nothing.' To imagine anything else was inviting heartbreak. She opened her notebook, rapped the table with her pen. 'Concentrate.'

Hope looked as if she might say more, but Flora jumped in. 'You're right. It's a big moment. Lots of changes for all of us. We have to do something to mark the moment.'

Aware that she was fighting a losing battle, Hope surrendered. 'Okay, but nothing that involves me wearing wings and an 'L' plate.'

'What about a night in a spa?' Flora suggested. 'We could have the works: face, nails, massage?'

'Plus good food and a glass or two of bubbly. Just the thing to set us all up for the big day.' Ally looked at Hope.

'That'll do.'

'Great. Now who are you going to invite?'

'Courtesy demands I ask Princess Anna.'

'Ask away. She and Carlo have engagements in London the weekend before the wedding so I think you'll be safe.'

Hope arched a brow. 'Pillow talk?'

'If you think I'd waste time talking about Princess Anna when I'm in bed with Fredrik, think again,' she said. 'But please forget that you heard that from me.'

'Lip zipped,' Flora said, grinning.

'Right. Invite Anna as a courtesy. What about Celina? She isn't going to have much fun babysitting the Dowager.'

'It's worse than that,' Hope said. 'Jonas completely lost the plot and asked Jack Masterson to be his best man. Her ex-husband,' she added when they both looked blank.

Both Ally and Flora sat for moment in stunned silence.

'Celina was married to Jack Masterson? *The* Jack Masterson?' Legendary guitarist and singer, front man for the rock group South Face?

'They all met in college in the US, apparently.'

'Right. Well let's hope that doesn't leak out before the day or there'll be an invasion of groupies that nothing will stop.'

'He'll be keeping a very low profile. No hotels. He'll be staying at Westonbury Court before the wedding.'

'So is Celina,' Ally pointed out. 'It doesn't matter how amicable their divorce was, that isn't going to be any fun for her. We need to make an effort to include her. Offer her an escape if she needs it.'

'Leave it to me,' Flora said. 'I'll think of something.'

★   ★   ★

Ally peeled off her rubber gloves for the last time. The wedding was taking place

251

in ten days and she would be spending every waking hour of them coping with the last-minute details. Not just the final details of the press PR campaign to launch *Becoming a Princess*, fending off last-minute incursions by the press, but the Wedding on the Green had been her idea; she had promised to handle the arrangements and she wanted to ensure that it ran like clockwork.

'I'm off, Jennifer.'

'Ally . . . We'll miss you so much. I'm sorry you won't be back after the wedding but I suppose you have job offers rolling in?'

Jennifer's smile didn't quite meet her eyes and there was a touch of gritted teeth behind it.

'I've been really grateful for the job, Jennifer, but it's time to move on.'

'Of course. There's just one last thing. Could you take this through to the snug?' She handed her a tray containing a small cafètiere, two cups, sugar and cream. 'There's someone waiting to see you.'

Fredrik . . .

Her head might know that whatever they had was temporary but her heart, leaping with something very like joy, clearly hadn't got the message. She took the tray, backed into the room but when she turned the man sitting by the window wasn't Fredrik. It was Steve Pike, the editor of *Celebrity*.

'Ally.' He stood up, a courtesy he would never have extended when she worked for him.

'Steve.' She put the tray down but remained standing, forcing him to do the same.

'You're looking well.'

Better than him, she thought. There were strain lines around his eyes that hadn't been there a few months ago. The comments in rival magazines, newspaper gossip columns, laughing at the fact that he'd fired the woman who was going to be a royal bridesmaid, speculation on how long he would last, were clearly taking their toll.

'It must be the clean country air.'

He nodded, oblivious to the barbed comment. 'You've been doing an amazing job for Miss Kennard. I'm very impressed.' She waited. 'You received a copy of the magazine featuring your royal bridesmaid blog?'

'Along with a dozen others.'

She'd put the tear sheet in the album she had created for Hope, and a photocopy in her own job-seeking portfolio, along with all the others she'd received. The other editors had received personal thank you notes and the promise of a copy of *Becoming a Princess* hot off the press — no one was getting an advance look except the newspaper paying a lot of money to run an excerpt along with a colour feature on San Michele on the day of the wedding.

The editor of *Celebrity* had been sent a printed acknowledgement.

'Won't you sit down, Ally?'

'I'm not stopping.'

Steve nodded and, accepting that this wasn't going to be a convivial chat over a cup of coffee, took a small piece of folded paper from his inside pocket and handed it to her.

She opened it and on it was written a life-changing sum of money. More than enough to move back to London and set herself up in her own PR business.

She didn't respond — she was literally speechless — but assuming that she was waiting for him to raise his offer, he took it back, crossed out the figure and increased it by twenty five per cent before handing it back.

'That's it. My best offer.'

She knew that kind of sum was paid for pictures, gossip, to run interference across a rival's expensive exclusive, but to see it in black and white was shocking.

'Photographs, details of the dress, the wedding menu, gossip,' he prompted.

Steve Pike was a man who thought everyone had a price and he was showing her the money, certain that she would not be able to resist all those noughts.

Not sure how steady her voice would be she tossed the paper on the table and walked out, desperate to get home and stand under a hot shower until she felt clean.

⋆　⋆　⋆

Fredrik, having organized security for the royal party in London, left them in the capable hands of his second in command and drove down to Wiltshire to check that everything was ready for their arrival.

It was still early and he pulled into the Three Bells car park, hoping to catch Ally in her granny's pinny.

'Fredrik . . . ' Jennifer Harmon was all smiles. 'Are you here to check us out before the wedding?'

'Not necessary, Mrs Harmon. I was hoping to catch Ally.'

'She is *such* a popular girl these days. The editor of *Celebrity* was in here a couple of days ago. I let them have the snug for their meeting. Can I get you anything? Coffee? A drink?'

'She's not here?'

'Oh, no, didn't I say? She doesn't have time to work here now. And of course she doesn't need the money. Today's edition,' she said, pushing an open copy of the magazine towards him.

It was folded back at a photograph of a page from the wedding diary.

He stared at it for a moment. 'Can I get a copy of this from the village store?'

She took a piece of paper from her pocket to mark the page, closed the magazine and offered it to him. 'Take this one.'

*   *   *

There were roses showering petals on the windowsill of the Hasebury Hall office. She was going to miss working here after the wedding, but for now there was plenty to keep her busy.

She was less than halfway through

her post when she opened an envelope containing a tear sheet from *Celebrity*. Apart from the headline all it contained was a photographic image of a page from the wedding diary.

For a moment she couldn't believe what she was seeing. Then she did and she couldn't breathe. Fredrik . . . He'd think that she'd sold out. That she'd been playing him . . . She had to speak to him before he saw it and she grabbed her phone and hit fast dial.

He wasn't picking up. She waited impatiently while he invited her to leave a message, then said, 'Fredrik — '

'Ally.'

She looked at her phone, frowned and then, sensing the presence behind her, spun round.

'Fredrik . . . You're here. I wasn't expecting you until after the weekend.'

12

'Obviously.'

There was no kiss, no smile as he took a step forward, pushed the door closed behind him and her initial jolt of pleasure at seeing him faded as he tossed the latest copy of *Celebrity* on her desk.

'You've seen it already. I'd hoped — '

'What? That I'd be too busy to notice?'

'No! I was just calling to let you know. Explain.'

'What? That someone leaked it?' He didn't wait, wasn't interested in hearing what she might have to say but swept on. 'You've played it so beautifully, Ally. All that crap about how Hope and Flora had rescued you from a groper in the dark. How you could never betray either of them.'

'It wasn't — '

'I knew it,' he said, not prepared to

listen to anything she had to say until he'd got it all off his chest. 'I knew it right from the start. You're out of a job, in debt and you had all the contacts. It was obvious that you'd have every creep running a gossip mag lining up to offer you money, a job. Common sense told me that you'd take it but one damn kiss and like everyone else I took the bait you threw me and swallowed it hook, line and sinker.'

He crossed to the window, staring out at the garden as if he couldn't bear to look at her, his hands thrust deep into his pockets as if he couldn't trust himself not to throttle her, his entire body vibrating with tension.

'Dom told you that I didn't speak to my mother and an hour later you were telling me how you'd confronted your worst fear, talked to your attacker and with one bound you were free . . . '

'Are you sorry you talked to your mother?'

He stiffened. 'No, but that's not the damn point.'

'I'm sure you'll get to it.'

He turned to face her. 'The point is, Ally, that you're brilliant at what you do. People trust you, confide in you. Even the Crown Princess melted for you.'

'I talked to her,' she said. 'Everyone else seems too scared to. She's an unhappy woman.'

He swore. 'You must have enough dirt to start your own gossip magazine.'

'Undoubtedly,' she said. 'Unhappy people talk to me. In the bus queue, on trains, sitting at the next table in a coffee shop. They always have. Nico spilled his heart out. Princess Anna told me how she married for duty but fell in love with her husband.'

'So why is she unhappy?'

'Because for him it was never more than duty and he's begun looking at other women with hungry eyes.'

He went white. 'She told you that?'

'No, I saw that. He's unhappy, too.'

'Is that what you sold to Steven Pike? Not just your friend's wedding, but hints of a royal scandal as well?'

'Steven?'

'You met him at the Three Bells.' He took a piece of paper from his pocket and held it out to her so that she could read the offers he'd made. His first crossed out for a higher sum.

'Jennifer gave you that.'

'Does it matter where I got it?'

She shook her head, because it didn't. If he believed that she'd taken the modern equivalent of thirty pieces of silver nothing mattered.

'You never asked why he sacked me, Fredrik.'

'I assumed staff cutbacks.'

'You didn't check to make sure I hadn't been pilfering the petty cash? Selling our scoops to other magazines?' He didn't answer. 'I struggled to find a job after university. I had planned to join the BBC or CNN and become a serious news journalist but the recession was biting deep and no one was hiring. I took whatever jobs I could get. The Three Bells kitchen isn't the first one I've cleaned.'

'So?'

'I was walking home late one night when I saw an old lady, well the worse for drink, sitting in the gutter. She was crying so I stopped and sat with her for a while. When she was able to stand I took her back to my bedsit, gave her tea and put her to bed.'

'If that's true you were taking a risk.'

'Not really. I'd recognized her.' She named a much-loved actress. 'The next morning she talked to me. She'd always had a drink problem, apparently. She'd managed to keep it under control but her beloved dog had died. Over breakfast she asked about my dreams and a week later I had a call from the editor of *Celebrity* — not Steven Pike, his predecessor, offering me job. Apparently he and the actress were old friends and she'd called him, asked him to give me a chance.'

'What's that — '

'Three years later I was at a wedding and I found the same woman slumped behind the marquee. I helped her into the hotel, found her a room so that she could sleep it off. A week later I was walked to the door with the contents of my desk drawer in a cardboard box.'

'What had changed?'

'The magazine had been taken over. Steve Pike was the new editor and the tone had been shifting downwards. Fewer high society weddings, more sleazy gossip.'

'You were sacked for helping her?'

'I was sacked because not only didn't I take a picture of her lying on the grass clutching an empty champagne bottle and send in the story but, far worse, someone else took a photograph of her being helped into the hotel by a 'good Samaritan' and sold it to *Glitz*.'

'And the meeting?'

'I'd been ignoring his calls so he turned up at the Three Bells a few days ago . . . ' She shook her head. 'He didn't get anything from me but apparently Jennifer had lifted that mock-up from my bag weeks before.'

She picked up the offending article and held it up for him to see. 'The photograph, in case you're actually interested, is me at my sixth birthday party.'

'Jennifer gave it to him?'

'I have only circumstantial evidence.'

He swore again. 'She made a point of telling me about you seeing Pike,' he said. 'She used that piece of paper as a bookmark. Why would she want to hurt you?'

She shrugged. 'Jealousy?'

'If you'd told me . . . '

'He made me an offer; I turned him down. Clearly I should have torn up that piece of paper but I didn't think it was important enough for such dramatics. If you knew me, if you trusted me, Fredrik, I wouldn't have to tell you that.'

'It's your job, Ally.'

His words echoed around the room like the clang of a stone hitting a bucket.

'It was.'

If he'd been listening he'd know that she'd never used her job to hurt people but, in the end, they were just words, meaningless without trust and they had both been short of that when it had mattered.

★ ★ ★

For a moment the only sound was that of a blackbird's lyrical song filling the garden. Not a love song but a male on the defensive, warning off other birds who might want to take over his territory.

They were all on the defensive, Fredrik thought as he looked at the picture of the little girl about to blow out the candles on her birthday cake, her dark hair cut in little fringe, big green-gold eyes smiling with excitement.

Convinced he'd been suckered by a woman playing a clever game, he'd barely glanced at it in the pub. Her face was no longer that round, she didn't have a gap in her teeth, but the smile was unmistakable.

The word he used was an old San Michele dialect, but the meaning was clear enough.

He'd flung back her own words to him, her reason for not telling him when Hope had needed time, space with Jonas to work through her future. The difference was that she'd been putting her friend — a woman she'd known since she was a child, a woman she loved — first.

He had allowed his natural cynicism to over-ride everything he knew, felt about Ally.

He was an idiot and if he lost her, he had no one but himself to blame.

'I'm so sorry, Ally. I barged in without giving you a chance to explain.'

'I'm sorry too, Fredrik.' Her tone was cool, not icy, merely studiedly indifferent.

'You didn't trust me,' he said, attempting to win back some ground, get back to where they were. He realized his mistake the moment the words were out of his mouth.

'So what are you suggesting?' she asked, and this time there was definitely ice. Thin, razor-sharp shards of ice in every word. 'That it's my turn to take you miles from anywhere and shag your brains out until you trust me?'

Trust. She'd told him that first night in San Michele that she had never used her job to hurt people but, in the end, they were just words, meaningless without trust and they had both been short of that when it had mattered.

With absolutely nothing left to lose he said, 'If that's an offer I'll take it.'

'Right now,' she said, 'I have more pressing problems.'

'Is there anything I can do to help?'

She told him in the minimum number of words about her hen party concerns. That if Jennifer had been through her bag and found the booking . . .

'I'll talk to her — '

'No! She's involved with catering the

Wedding on the Green. Getting that sorted without offending anyone has taken diplomacy to a whole new level.'

'And Steven Pike?'

'He'd just deny all knowledge.'

'What the devil do you want me to do, then?'

'Your job.'

'In that case you'll have to tell me what's involved.'

'A dozen friends having facials, nail jobs, good food and champagne. I'll email you the list for your security officers.'

'Is it an overnight stay?'

'No. It's just from eight o'clock until midnight. Anyone who's coming a long distance is staying at the Hall.'

The phone rang, rescuing her from this nightmare conversation. Ally answered, picked it, said, 'One moment.' Then, holding it to her chest, she said, 'Is that all?'

Fredrik didn't move for what seemed like a year, but then he turned and walked out.

Ally twitched at the quiet click as the

door closed behind him then sucked in a long, painful breath, lifted the phone, her voice very nearly breaking as she said, 'Mum . . . '

'Ally? Are you okay?'

'Fine,' she said, grabbing a tissue to catch the flow of tears pouring down her face. 'I'm fine. What can I do for you?'

'I just had a call from your Aunt Celia. Apparently there's a picture of you on your sixth birthday in this week's *Celebrity*.'

She sniffed, managed a half laugh. 'I know. I'm just going to tweet Steve Pike and let him know how thrilled I am.'

* * *

Fredrik drove back to Westonbury Court barely conscious of how he'd got there. How could his life have taken a nosedive over a cliff in the space of a couple of hours? If he'd gone straight to the Hall, or to her home . . .

How could he have been so crass?

Okay, so he'd been hurt that she hadn't trusted him enough to tell him that Hope and Jonas had disappeared, but she'd been protecting her friend. That's what she always did. She'd protected Nico when, his tongue loosened by an excess of champagne, he'd unburdened himself to her. She'd protected that old actress. She hadn't needed the wedding; she'd kept heaven alone knew how many secrets that could have made her a fortune. Instead she'd been cleaning Jennifer Harmon's kitchen for a pittance.

One thing was certain. If you weren't sure about the future, losing it certainly focused the mind.

★ ★ ★

Ally had turned off her phone's ringtone as she walked the green with the village groundsman on Friday morning, discussing the final details of the layout of the marquee, dance floor, bandstand and carousel for the Wedding on the Green.

He'd done it all a dozen times before for the village fete and, once she realized she was just there to nod and say yes, she handed over the list of stallholders and told him to get on with it.

With nothing demanding her attention for the next ten minutes, she crossed to the bench where she and Fredrik had talked that first night.

She took out her phone, not sure whether she wanted there to be a text from Fredrik or whether she never wanted to hear from him again. The heart-drop when there was nothing was answer enough.

She leaned back against the bench remembering that night. How he'd encouraged her to talk — ironic in the circumstances. How, conscious of her fear, he'd kissed her hand when any other man would have gone for the kind of goodnight kiss that would have kept the neighbours gossiping for weeks. She was pretty sure that she'd fallen in love with him right there.

Her phone rang. Number withheld. Another journalist wanting a 'quote' from the royal bride-to-be, no doubt.

'Ally Parker.'

'I just wanted you to know that you can go ahead with your spa party.'

She wanted to ask him how he could be sure. The words were on the tip of her tongue but she clamped her teeth shut before they could escape. If he wasn't sure, he wouldn't have phoned her. She took a deep breath.

'Thank you, Fredrik.'

'I'm just doing my job. Someone will be there to keep an eye on things but you won't know they're there. Have a good time.'

'Fredrik . . . ' But he was gone.

Number withheld? Did he think she wouldn't answer if she knew it was him?

She sighed, called Flora to let her know that their emergency backup plan, a pizza and Prosecco party at the Hall, wouldn't be needed. She never felt less like a party but she went home to get ready.

Her father dropped her off at the spa at seven-thirty, so that she could check that everything was in place, take some photographs of the champagne standing in ice buckets, of the pool, still and inviting in the soft lighting, the array of nail colours for her Facebook page and blog.

The manager offered to accompany her, show her around, but she wanted a few minutes on her own, a moment of quiet but when she entered the spa there was a member of staff checking something in one of the treatment rooms. Or maybe not.

Security had checked the place, but what if someone . . . Her heart stopped as she walked in and came face to face with Fredrik.

'I'm sorry. I planned to be out of here — '

'I'm early,' she said, not wanting him to apologize for doing his job. She made an awkward little gesture — this was so cringe-makingly embarrassing. 'I wanted to check that everything was in place.'

'We're both obsessive about the details.' He held up the gadget he was holding. 'I was doing one last sweep for bugs.'

'Did you find anything?'

'Not this time.'

'And last time?' she asked, her heart sinking.

'They are safely locked away in my car. Every room in the place has been checked in the last hour. I've spoken to the staff, explained that whatever they've been paid is of no interest to me, but they will be scanned before they enter the spa and anyone found carrying a recording device will be dismissed on the spot.'

'That's how you found them? Using a scanner.' She sighed. 'I shouldn't have tweaked Steve Pike's nose on Twitter . . . '

'This isn't about anything you've done, Ally. He would have done this anyway.' He took another device from his pocket that looked exactly like a smart phone. 'This is a spare.' He turned it on and, a tiny green light briefly appeared and then went out. 'It's on. Keep it with you and if there's the slightest peep out of it, give me a call.'

'You're leaving?'

'No. I'll be here all evening in case whoever planted these turns up to see why he's not getting any pictures.'

'Thank you.'

'I'm just doing my job.'

She shook her head. 'Your job is to keep the royal family safe. Why are you here when you should be in London with Prince Carlo and Princess Anna?'

'I'm tired of hauling Nico out of nightclubs, watching royal backs.'

'Carrying their coats? Figuratively speaking,' she added.

He nodded. 'I've done my duty. It's time to move on.'

'You're leaving the palace? What will they do without a Jensson to guard their backs?'

'My successor is taking care of things in London. I'm just staying to back him out at the wedding.'

'What will you do? Have you made any plans?'

'Something bigger,' he said. 'Hope is looking for someone to head up her charity. Jonas asked if I would be interested.'

Hope for Children . . .

Hope's charity would provide support for children who look after their younger siblings and sick or disabled parents. Fredrik must have seen so much of that serving with UN forces in war zones. He'd have personal experience of the problem, understand what was needed.

'That's certainly bigger,' she said. 'Are you? Interested.'

'Maybe — ' The sound of laughter reached them from the entrance and he looked up. 'Your party has arrived.'

The only party she wanted at that moment was standing right in front of her but she just nodded.

'What do you want me to do with the evidence?'

Evidence?

'I took photographs of them in situ but maybe you should hang on to the hardware.'

'Oh, yes. Definitely one for the blog.'

'Be careful what you say.'

'I won't mention any names. I won't have to.' She slipped the scanner into her pocket. 'Could you bring it over to the Hall tomorrow morning? Not too early.' He nodded, but as he headed for the door she called after him, 'Fredrik . . .' He paused, looked back. 'If someone does turn up, call me.'

'What will you do?'

'Scare him to death with my facemask.'

And finally she got a smile.

13

Fredrik hadn't called but when Max turned up to pick up Flora and Hope and a couple of women who were staying over at the Hall, Ally found him in the hotel lobby, still keeping an eye on things.

Ally went to sit by him for a moment. 'You look exhausted. When did you last sleep?'

'It's been a while,' he said. 'Did you have a good time?'

'Yes, thanks to you.'

'Ally? Are you coming,' Flora called from the door.

'You're not fit to drive, Fredrik. Do you want Max to run you back to Westonbury Court?'

'No need. I've got a room here.'

'Ally?'

'No thanks, Flora. I'm good.'

She laughed. 'Oh, don't be good,

darling. After all your hard work you deserve to be very, very bad. See you tomorrow.'

★ ★ ★

Fredrik woke just as it was getting light and discovered that Ally was beside him, her hair spread over his pillow, her hand looped over his waist.

He closed his eyes, opened them again and she was still there. Not a figment of his imagination.

As he propped himself on his elbow so that he could look at her, watch her sleeping, her hand slipped to his thigh and every cell in his body responded to the slide of her fingers over his skin.

He didn't disturb her; sleeping beside a man demonstrated a trust far greater than anything given in the rush of sex and he treasured the moment for a while before bending to touch her lips with a barely there kiss.

'Hey there, Prince Charming,' she said, opening her eyes. 'I'm Cinderella, remember, not Sleeping Beauty.'

'You weren't asleep.'

'How did you know?'

He could have told her that when she was asleep he could see her eyes move beneath the lids as she dreamed, that there was a vulnerability that she concealed when she was awake.

'The corner of your mouth twitched,' he said. 'Your hand moved.'

Not the unconscious slide of a hand slipping out of control but a teasing, come and get me touch.

'Busted,' she said, grinning as she turned in to him, taking him firmly in hand, returning his kiss with interest and then, when he was struggling for breath, she pushed him onto his back and straddled him.

'What did I do to deserve this?' he asked.

'You kept watch over us all night so I returned the favour and kept watch over you.'

'That's all you did?'

'You were asleep before I brushed my teeth.'

'I'm awake now.'

'I noticed.'

He reached for her, but she slapped his hands away.

'Men always think that sex is about them,' she said, lowering her mouth to his and taking possession of it in a long intimate kiss and when she looked up her eyes were blazing like hot emeralds. 'You heard Flora. This is my reward for all my hard work.'

'Help yourself . . . ' was all he managed before she took her mouth on a slow, tormenting exploration of his body. Mouth, tongue, teeth . . . Her breasts brushing against his chest, his stomach . . .

He groaned as her lips enclosed the only thinking part of him and she smiled like a kitten being offered a bowl of cream.

She was driving him crazy and she knew it. He wanted to seize her, bury himself in her, make her his in every possible way but she'd made it plain that she was in charge.

Right now she could have whatever she wanted . . .

It had been her choice to stay but he had no sense that she'd forgiven him, that this was not only her pleasure but his punishment for not trusting her. Punishment suggested the possibility of redemption and, clutching the sheet he was lying on to stop himself from reaching for her, he lay back and he took it until later, much later, she stopped torturing him and invited him to the party.

They had breakfast in bed, then lunch until somewhere in the middle of the afternoon she stepped out of the shower they'd shared and instead of heading back to bed she wrapped a towel around herself and dried her hair.

He leaned against the bathroom door watching her concentrate as she used brush and dryer to smooth it into dark silken strands that floated around her naked shoulders.

'Thank you.' She looked up at him. 'For staying.'

She gave the tiniest of shrugs. 'It was my pleasure,' she said as if it was all about sex, about a modern young woman taking casual pleasure, but there was a touch of colour in her cheekbones. 'When are the royal party arriving?'

'Tomorrow.'

'Shouldn't you be there?'

'I was needed here. Can we have dinner tonight?'

'Not tonight. We all thought Celina seemed a bit isolated. She didn't want to come to the hen party but we wanted to include her so we're having a picnic in the grounds of Hasebury Hall.'

'That's thoughtful. Tomorrow?'

'Won't you be busy?'

'Captain Lukas is handling close protection this weekend.'

'Okay . . . Well, I'll be busy in the morning, but there's a cricket match in the afternoon. The Earl's team are playing Combe St Philip. It's a local fixture going back to the eighteenth century.'

'Cricket?'

'National game. Two teams, eleven on each side. The team who makes the most runs wins.'

'I thought football was your national game.'

'We play that in the winter.'

'Right.'

'Dad will be umpiring for the village team and there will be afternoon tea.'

He grinned. 'Tea?'

'It's traditional,' she said, but she was grinning now, too. 'Cucumber sandwiches, scones, strawberries, cake. The pub will be open for those who prefer a beer with their Victoria sandwich.'

'Then cricket it is.'

He ran her home, parking in the Three Bells car park so that he could walk her to her door. 'This isn't necessary,' she protested.

'Yes, it is.' He took her arm and when she opened the front door, he didn't stand on the doorstep saying he'd see her tomorrow, but followed her in.

'Fredrik . . . ' Ally's mother greeted

him with the caution of a mother whose daughter has been brought home by a man she's undoubtedly spent the night with. 'How lovely to see you again.'

'Hello, Debbie.' She blushed with pleasure, turning as her husband came in from the kitchen. 'I don't think you've met my husband. George, this is Count Fredrik Jensson.'

'Just Fredrik. Mr Parker.' He offered his hand. 'Good to finally meet you. I'm looking forward to the cricket match tomorrow.'

Ally covered a splutter with a cough.

George Parker paused for a moment to look him in the eye, weigh him up before he took his hand with a nod that seemed to signal acceptance.

'Can I get you a cup of coffee, Fredrik?' Debbie asked.

'That would be most welcome. Perhaps we could use your dining room table? Ally wants to take some photographs of these before I take them to Westonbury Court and lock them away in the gun room.'

'What have you got there?' George asked.

'Surveillance devices, Dad,' Ally said. 'Fredrik found them and stayed at the spa to take care of us last night.'

'That dreadful man Pike?' her mother asked.

'It seems likely.'

'Then we'll have cake to sweeten our mouths.'

Fredrik grinned. 'I was hoping you'd say that.'

Ally raised an eyebrow at him, but she wasn't the only one who knew how to charm the birds from the trees.

An hour later, she walked him to the Market Cross. 'What was all that about?'

'Did you know,' he said, 'that Prince Charming, disguised as his valet, had met Cinderella long before the ball?' he said. 'Gathering wood in the forest, wearing nothing but rags. That was when he fell in love with her.'

'Is this your way of breaking it to me that you have a rubber glove fixation?'

'It's my way of telling you that I'm

not looking for a princess, but someone with the courage to take on whatever life throws at her, principles that never waver.' He didn't wait for her to respond. 'I'll pick you up tomorrow at twelve. If I'm going to spend an entire afternoon watching a game I know nothing about I am going to need lunch first.'

* * *

'Okay, spill,' Hope demanded.

The sun had set, twilight was deepening and Hope, Flora and Celina were already stretched out in front of the gothic cottage, a picturesque folly built by a Victorian Kennard.

It was stone, with little arched windows and smothered with pink roses and tiny, solar-powered lights. They'd chosen the spot for their picnic because it had been Hope and Ally's secret hangout when they were teens, their special place, and today they wanted to share it with Flora and Celina.

'Spill?'

'I've been trying to get hold of you most of the day. What happened last night?'

'Nothing.'

'Nothing?'

'Fredrik was exhausted,' she said. 'Asleep before I'd brushed my teeth.'

'You have got to be kidding.'

Celina, eyebrows raised, said, 'You spent the night with Fredrik? I thought you weren't . . .' She stopped, clearly embarrassed. 'I saw him the other evening,' she admitted. 'He looked upset and when I asked him what was wrong he told me he'd made a mess of things.'

'He did, but he's making a serious effort to redeem himself.'

'So you're good?' Celina asked.

'We're working on it,' she said. 'We're having lunch tomorrow and then he's spending the afternoon at the cricket match.'

'Ally!' Flora exclaimed, opening a second bottle of Prosecco. 'I am fairly certain that the Court of Human Rights considers that cruel and unusual punishment for anyone who hasn't been brought up playing the game.'

'I did tell him that forgiveness might require his bloody heart on a plate,' Celina said.

Ally joined in the laughter but she was only half there as she listened while Celina, becoming more relaxed under the influence of Flora's home-made pizza and good wine, told them about how she'd met Jack, his heroics in rescuing her from a man who didn't understand the meaning of the word 'no'. But when Flora and Hope responded with the story of her own incident in the car park Ally said, 'I talked to him.'

'Who?' Hope asked.

'That boy in the car park. Well, man. A few weeks ago.'

'Ally!'

'That first night, when Fredrik walked me home, something spooked me and I told him what had happened.'

Flora was about to say something,

but Hope put out a hand and stopped her. 'Go on.'

'I realized then that I was still emotionally crippled by that moment. That, if I didn't do something about it, I always would be.'

'What happened, Ally? When you saw him?'

'He cried . . . ' She sighed. 'Not everything is the way it seems. Sometimes we're so blocked by what has happened, or what we thought happened, that we can't see the truth.'

Like Fredrik with his mother. Like his response to the diary page in *Celebrity* . . . She realized that everyone was staring at her.

'Is there any more of that Prosecco?'

Later, after they'd waved Celina off, Hope said, 'Can you spare an hour tomorrow, Ally? There's something I want to ask you.'

'There's nothing wrong?'

'No, no . . . It's not about the wedding. It's about the charity.'

'Of course. About ten?'

291

She nodded and Flora said, 'I'll walk you home.'

'No,' she said. 'No need. I'm fine.'

She hugged them both and then, as she walked home, she took out her phone and, about to text Fredrik, she called him instead.

'What are you doing?' she asked.

'I had a drink with Nico and Jack then got called out because someone was spotted in the woods at Westonbury Court.'

'A poacher?'

'A courting couple.'

'Oh dear. Awkward.'

'I could have done without it. Did you have a good time?'

'Yes, thanks. I'm walking home now. On my own.'

'Ally — '

'I'm fine,' she said. 'I'm only calling because Mum's cooking roast beef tomorrow and it'll be a lot better than anything we'll get in a pub.'

'Are you asking me to have lunch with your family?'

'Only if you want to.'

There was a pause as he thought about it and she panicked. It was too much, too soon . . .

'I . . . yes. Thank you. I'd love to come.'

'You still have to go to the cricket match afterwards,' she warned, in an effort to downplay the importance of such an invitation.

'I've been reading up on it. I have some of the fielding terms — silly mid-off, cover point, slip — but what the heck is a googly? And the Duckworth Lewis system?'

She just laughed. 'I'm home now. See you tomorrow.'

She was grinning as she rang off. It was impossible not to love a man who was trying so hard. Foolish, a heart-breaker for sure, but impossible.

* * *

Fredrik drove into Ayesborough on Sunday morning and bought good red wine to go with the beef and a box of candied fruit and flowers for Debbie Parker. He turned up on Ally's doorstep on the dot of twelve.

George answered the door, took the wine and waved him through to the kitchen where a pink-faced Debbie was basting a good-looking piece of beef and Ally was mixing something with an electric hand whisk. 'Don't come any nearer,' she warned, fending him off one-handed as he got nearer. 'You'll get splattered.'

George, having opened the wine and set it on the side to breathe, said, 'Leave them to it. It's opening time.'

Fredrik glanced at Ally, who just grinned and said, 'It's traditional.'

He half expected to be grilled about his intentions, but instead they played darts, drank a rich, nutty local ale and walked back to the cottage discussing the likelihood of rain making a mess of the wedding.

Lunch was, as Ally had promised, a treat. Rare beef, golden roast potatoes, a towering pillow of Yorkshire pudding and creamed horseradish hot enough to make your eyes water.

Conversation was mostly Debbie talking about the wedding but Ally caught his eye from time to time and he had a vision of Sundays like this stretching into the future. A family sitting around a table, relaxed, content, with Ally there when he looked up, smiling at him.

There were strawberries from the garden, served with clotted cream and crisp, sugary little pastries to follow and then coffee.

'Debbie, that was wonderful,' he said. 'Can I do anything to help?'

'No, dear. You all go off to the match. I'll come along later.'

'If you're sure . . . '

Ally gave him a quick nod. 'Mum is a bit OCD about her kitchen,' she said, as they followed George down to the village green. 'She allows me to help with the cooking, but no one else is capable of cleaning up to her standard.'

'But — '

'She's happy.'

'Are you happy?'

She looked momentarily disconcerted and for once there was no quick comeback. Then she said, 'That depends on who wins this match.' She looked across at the centre of the pitch. 'It looks like we've won the toss.'

'Which means?'

'We get to choose whether to bat or field first. It looks as if we're batting.'

'Is that good?'

'We'll get the best of the wicket. Of course if it rains — '

He looked up, hopefully.

She laughed. 'It's not going to rain,' she said, catching his hand and pulling him towards a couple of empty deck-chairs but before they reached them his phone rang. 'Did you get someone to ring and rescue you? Your chum Celina, perhaps?'

He held the phone up so that she could see it was Prince Carlo calling and then walked away.

⋆   ⋆   ⋆

Ally sighed but was quickly joined by a group of locals wanting the latest gossip on the wedding, until things started to hot up on the field and their attention shifted. Fredrik caught her eye, gave an apologetic shrug. Just like dating a cop, she thought, but left him to get on with whatever crisis had blown up, turning at a shout of dismay as their opening bat was dismissed for a duck.

'Out for duck? What the heck does that mean?'

She turned at the American accent and her heart did a little bounce. 'It means he didn't score. At all,' she said, offering him her hand. 'Jack Masterson. How d'you do?'

'Ally Parker, right? Nico pointed you out.'

'He's here? Lock up the local maidens!'

'I understand you're a journalist. I thought maybe you'd like a chat?'

For a moment she didn't think she'd

heard that right. 'You're offering me an interview?'

'*South Face* are going on tour after the wedding but there are going to be changes.'

'Oh ... ' She turned as Fredrik reappeared at her side, phone nowhere to be seen and took her hand. 'Have you met Fredrik Jensson?' she asked.

Jack nodded, acknowledging him. 'We ran into one another in the pub last night. He said that if I wanted to talk to the press you're a journalist who can be trusted.'

Fredrik had said that? Unable to look at him, she laced her fingers through his.

Forgiven. Totally forgiven.

'When do you think you'll have a moment?'

'The TV people are setting up tomorrow, Jack. I need to be at the church to make sure they stick to what Hope and Jonas have agreed. Maybe Tuesday?'

They fixed a time, chatted for a few

minutes and then she tugged Fredrik away.

'Where are we going?'

'You set me up to interview Jack Masterson. You are totally excused from cricket,' she said.

'You're a fan?' he asked, glaring back over his shoulder to where Jack was chatting to some of the villagers.

'I had a poster of him on my bedroom wall. The moody one, all shadows and black leather,' she said, unable to resist teasing him a little. 'I still have it somewhere.'

He muttered something under his breath and she laughed. 'I'm not a star-struck teenager any more, Fredrik.'

'It's not only teenagers — '

She stopped. 'I'm not a teenager,' she repeated and because for some words the moment came and if you didn't say them you'd regret it. Always. 'I'm a woman. And I'm in love.' No, that wasn't enough. 'I'm in love with you.'

14

Fredrik had taken another step but he spun round to face her.

The arctic grey eyes of that first morning had warmed to molten silver, the poker face had become so familiar that she could read every nuance of emotion; right now it was concern and she reached out, cradled his cheek in her palm, wanting to reassure him.

'I expect nothing, demand nothing. I just wanted you to know.'

'Ally — '

'Alice . . . ' Her throat hurt in the way it did when you were about to cry and her voice was hoarse with emotion as she said, 'My name is Alice.'

He seemed lost for words. Not sure if it was in a good way or it was all simply too much, she took a step back. 'It doesn't mean . . . I don't expect . . . ' she said again, stumbling over the words, afraid that she had broken something too new to be tested. But then he said it.

'Alice . . . ' A song, a prayer, something more that she'd never heard in those two syllables before. 'My own dear, lovely Alice. You can expect, demand of me anything . . . '

And stepping after her he took her in his arms and kissed her. No longer an exploration of the new, not a passionate prelude to sex but two people recognizing in each other a new beginning. Setting out on a journey and, as they broke apart, they both said —

'I have something to tell you . . . '

'I have something to tell you . . . '

'You first,' Fredrik said.

'Hope needs someone to create the public face of her charity, do the PR, show the world what's needed, what Hope for Children is doing. She's asked me if I'd like the job.'

'And would you?'

'It's about as special as it gets. Telling the world what's happening, making a difference. There'll be two offices. One here at Hasebury Hall but the other will be in San Michele. In the palace. But you know that . . . ' She broke off. 'Jonas has already asked you to head it up.'

'Are you saying that if I wasn't happy with that you'd turn down your dream job?'

She'd have to. She couldn't see him every day and not be with him.

'What were you going to say?' she asked.

'That it's not a problem. I've reached a point in my life where I want to do more with my life than haul Nico out of nightclubs, chase trespassers out of the castle grounds — '

'Save hen parties from prying reporters?'

He grinned. 'That mission was a one-off and it came with benefits.'

She gave him a shove with her shoulder and he put his arm around her, drew her close. 'Behave,' he said. 'This is important.'

She suddenly realized exactly what he was telling her. He wanted more than to head up a small charity. 'You're moving on.'

'Not far. I'll still have an office in the palace although I don't envisage spending much time there.'

'So it wouldn't matter if I was there?' Because the likelihood of their paths crossing was minimal?

'It matters,' he said, fiercely, 'because we'll be sharing those two offices. In the palace. At Hasebury Hall.'

'I don't . . . '

'I told you that Jonas and Hope asked me if I'd head up Hope for Children. I've been in the field, seen the need but I had commitments . . . The call from Prince Carlo was to let me know that Princess Anna is happy with Captain Lukas and he's agreed to release me with immediate effect.'

'What?' There were tears in her eyes but she was laughing, too. 'Did Jonas tell you they were asking me?'

'They said they wanted you but they

knew we were involved, that it might be awkward. They said it was my call.'

'And you said yes?'

'They want people they know, people they trust.'

That word again . . .

'Yes.'

'That was before you thought I'd betrayed everyone. Do you still want me?'

'Alice . . . ' He smiled as he said her name, took her hand. 'There comes a moment in life when going solo loses its appeal. For me that moment arrived when I met you. I'm training with the mountain rescue team; I'm building bridges with my family. I will take on the role of director of Hope for Children because it's important to me, but with you at my side it will be a joy. Will you join me?'

Her answer was silent but eloquent as they sealed their partnership with a kiss that was only disturbed by a shout from the field behind them.

Fredrik looked up. 'The game appears

to be hotting up. If I'm going to be spending time here I'd better find out what it's all about.'

'Forget the cricket,' she said, as he put his arm around her and they walked back to the green. 'They'll be serving tea soon and that's the best part.'

* * *

Monday passed in a blur as the church was cleaned and polished from apse to font, the volunteers taking no nonsense from the San Michele TV crew who had arrived with a list of demands as long as her arm.

With Fredrik's help, she confined them to the organ loft and a perch erected opposite but just out of sight of the great west door inside the church, and one cherry picker, tucked away behind the trees.

Marquees were being erected in the Hall grounds — which was nothing to do with her — and on the Green, which was. A wooden dance floor was finally levelled and, by evening, everything was set up and she fell into bed exhausted.

On Tuesday it rained.

The royal party, hurrying into church under vast umbrellas for the rehearsal, were heard muttering about English weather. Obviously, the sun was shining its heart out in San Michele.

Fredrik was there taking care of the royals, and stepped in to take the pictures she needed since she would be in some of them. He stole a brief kiss in the vestry when he handed over her camera before they both had to be somewhere else.

Jack Masterson hadn't turned up for some reason and Nico was standing in for him. Celina left in the middle of the rehearsal but apart from that everything went as it should.

The rain had stopped by six, leaving everything sparkling clean in the evening sunshine and everyone's mood had lifted by the time they sat down for the rehearsal dinner.

The table layout had Fredrik on the far side of the table and at the other end. When she went to sit down, however, his name card was beside hers.

'You switched!' she whispered.

'It was a security issue.' She must have looked sceptical because he said, 'I felt insecure with you sitting next to Nico.'

She laughed. 'Idiot.'

'So you keep saying and yet here I am, next to you. I must be doing something right.'

It felt very right sitting next to him, his shoulder touching hers and, while they engaged with everyone around them, once in a while their hands touched, fingers briefly entwined.

Afterwards, he saw her home, kissed her goodnight at her front door like they did in old movies — although her dad didn't appear to chase him away.

He leaned his forehead against hers. 'I'll see you tomorrow.'

'It's going to be crazy.'

'It'll be crazy until the reception but once the formalities are over I'm done, so save the first dance for me.'

'Just the first dance?'

'Does there have to be more than one? I've booked a hotel room.'

'I'll be asleep before you've brushed your teeth.'

'But when you wake up I'll be there. That's what love is all about. Not sex. It's being there.'

And right there, on the doorstep, Ally melted.

★　★　★

Ally's morning was all about the Wedding on the Green. She took photographs of everything and everyone for a souvenir album on the village website.

Villagers brought flowers to decorate the marquee. Great white feathery bunches of cow parsley, tall pink spires of rose bay willow herb from the hedgerows. Foxgloves, sunflowers, love in a mist, roses, clove-scented dianthus from their gardens.

Her mother's WI team were there, setting them up in buckets, giving everything a wonderful country fair feel.

The tables were laid with gorgeous cupcake posies waiting to be uncovered at the centre of every table.

Jennifer stiffened as she stopped to take a snapshot of her unpacking glasses as she and Pete set up the bar.

'Relax, Jennifer. It's going to be a wonderful day. Enjoy it.'

'I . . . Yes . . . Thank you,' she said and Pete Harmon, who'd donated enough Prosecco to float a battleship, threw her a grateful smile.

Her father had mustered the darts team to deliver the specially made gold wristbands — inscribed with 'Hope and Jonas — Combe St Philip' and the date — to everyone who was coming to the party. There were red ones for those who'd been lucky in the draw for the limited space in the churchyard for a close-up view of the arrival of the royal party and the bride.

Lunch was a snatched bite out of a sandwich and then she joined Flora and Hope at Hasebury Hall for the whole hair, make-up and getting dressed party.

There was a photographer to take official pictures once they were ready, but they all took pictures of each other, laughing, thoughtful, aware that nothing was ever going to be quite the same again.

She captured one of Hope, ready for church in a stunningly simple white lace dress that draped in a deep arc of soft folds from her shoulders. 'All anyone sees of the bride in church is her back,' Hope said. 'Better give them something interesting to look at.'

There was no train to drag on the path as she walked to church, no veil for the breeze to tease, just the sparkle of diamonds in her hair.

She was looking out of her bedroom window and the sun, slanting in sideways, was catching her hair so that the red glowed like fire, throwing her face into shadows. She looked serene. Every inch the princess she hadn't wanted to become. It was just a moment and then, as Max knocked and put his head around the door, she turned and smiled. And Ally caught that image, too.

'Is it time?'

In answer the church bells started to ring a joyful peal and Max said, 'They're playing your tune.'

She and Flora gathered up the little bridesmaids and pages who'd been in another room where Holly's mother and the royal children's nanny had been getting them ready, and ushered them down the drive and along the path, lined by villagers, to the church.

The young bridesmaids, Max's daughter and one of the little princesses, were wearing pale gold voile dresses with a dark red sash and dark red rosebuds in their hair, the San Michele colours, and they were greeted by a single 'Ahhh . . .'

The boys, remarkably well-behaved

but then they were royal princes and presumably knew what was expected of them, were in dark red breeches and gold and red waistcoats.

She and Flora were wearing the same dark red. Simple strapless princess-line dresses that would be perfect for dancing later that evening but for the church they were wearing elegant little matching boleros with elbow-length sleeves and stand-up collars to cover their shoulders.

Everyone had their cameras and phones out taking snaps and videos and, for a moment, Ally managed to forget that there was a TV cameraman, perched fifty feet up in a cherry picker, sending the images direct to San Michele.

As they entered the churchyard she caught sight of Fredrik. He was talking into a two-way radio but paused for a moment, absolutely still as he watched her walk towards him. Then they were around the church in the cool shade of the porch.

The clapping, in the distance at first

and then nearer and nearer, heralded the approach of Hope on Max's arm. The look that passed between Max and Flora as they arrived left her struggling with a sudden lump in her throat and she bent to shake out Hope's hem while Flora lined up the children behind her.

'Everyone ready?' the verger asked as the incidental music that Laura Chase had been playing stopped and the church became quiet.

Max glanced around, smiled at the children. 'All ready,' he said.

The verger gave a signal, there was a rustle as the congregation stood and the first sweet notes of 'Dance of the Blessed Spirits' filled the church. Max glanced at his sister, she nodded and then, to a sigh that filled the church, Hope walked down the aisle to her waiting prince.

The service was moving, special. The Dowager nodded as they took their vows, a lace handkerchief appeared in Princess Anna's hand while poor Nico, clearly anticipating pressure to man up

313

and follow suit, could hardly bear to look.

The register was signed and then they were all back out in the sunshine, bells ringing, villagers flinging rose petals, while a woman from the local photographic club used Ally's camera to capture the moment when Hope and Jonas paused under the lychgate for a traditional kiss.

Ally retrieved the camera, and climbed into the waiting car to race back to the Hall and get one to the printer. She knew without looking that it was Fredrik behind the wheel and put out a hand to acknowledge him as she flipped through the images looking for just one that would be perfect.

It was hard to choose from such a joyful collection but by the time they reached the Hall she had it. She turned to Fredrik to show him and realized that he was looking at her with just the same expression that she'd seen on Max's face when he was looking at Flora.

'How was it?' he asked.

'Um . . . ' She unstuck her tongue from the roof of her mouth. 'Simple. Moving. Perfect . . . '

'Just what Hope wanted, then.'

'Mmmm.'

And when she didn't move. 'Isn't there someone waiting for that?'

'Yes . . . ' She wanted to stay there. Wanted the rest of the day to be just the two of them and without thinking she leaned forward and kissed him. 'First dance . . . '

'Last dance,' he called after her as she ran into the house.

★   ★   ★

The reception was perfect. Flora's fabulous canapes, then the menu she'd created, supervising chefs she'd worked with in London right up until the minute she sat down. The speeches were not too long. Max's was moving. Jack was funny; Prince Carlo charm itself.

Fredrik, who'd handed over to Captain Lukas immediately after the service, was sitting at a table with her parents, the vicar and his wife and the chairwoman of the parish council. They all seemed to be having a good time and when he caught her eye, he grinned.

It seems hours later when they watched Hope and Jonas take their first dance, swinging around the floor as if there was no one else in the room, before Fredrik turned to her. 'First dance, Alice . . . And the last?'

'Behave yourself,' she said. 'Bridesmaids have to dance with the groomsmen first,' she said, waltzing off with Nico until Fredrik could stand it no longer.

'Alice . . . '

Nico frowned. 'Alice? Why does he call you that?'

'Because he's earned the right,' she said, looking not at Nico, but the man she loved, before stepping into his arms.

They did their duty until Hope announced that she and Jonas were joining the Wedding on the Green.

They followed, touring the sideshows

where Fredrik won her a teddy on the shooting range. They rode on the carousel, ate *porchetta* and danced to the local band before finally slipping away into the night.

'How soon can you come to San Michele?' he asked as they headed to the Hall to pick up her overnight bag.

'I don't know. I've a million things to do tomorrow. I've got to update my blog — I should be doing that now instead of sneaking off to spend the night with you. I have to check that all the interviews with Hope and book previews made the papers . . . '

'And if they didn't what could you do about it?'

She gave a little shrug, laughed. 'Not a thing.'

'I know there will still be stuff you need to do to wrap things up but what I'm asking is do you have to be here?'

'Fredrik . . . ' Ally's heart was suddenly pounding like the beat of the drums still rocking the village green. 'What are you saying?'

317

'I'm saying that I'm not a youth, Alice. I'm a man and I'm not interested in a your place or mine relationship. I have an apartment overlooking the harbour in Liburno. I'm in love with you and I want you to be there every night, want to be with you every morning when I wake up.' He reached for her, drew her close. 'Say the word and I'll change that to 'we'.'

'We?'

'We have an apartment overlooking the harbour with the kind of internet access the inhabitants of this village can only dream about. The royal jet will be leaving after lunch tomorrow. Say the word and we could both be on it, starting our journey in style.'

'What's the word?'

'Yes.'

She laughed, threw her arms around his neck.

'I want to be with you, Fredrik, with or without your internet access. So yes, yes and yes. Tomorrow after lunch I'll be packed and ready and go but let's not waste another moment of tonight talking about it.'

* * *

It was so hot that when she breathed in the air was searing her lungs, but Ally couldn't be sure whether it was sweat or tears drying on her face.

Taking photographs of these children who were carers, helping their parents who were victims of landmines, who had terrible burns or were too sick to take care of themselves, seemed like an intrusion, a violation.

She looked up and saw Fredrik sitting with some of the older children, saw him put his arm around a child who should be at school but instead was looking after his younger siblings. Children that Hope for Children was offering a future.

She carried on taking photographs, talking to the children, their parents and grandparents until, wrung out, she ground to a halt, unable to carry on.

Fredrik joined her, took her hand as if he knew and as she turned in to him, her face in his shoulder, there was no doubt. They were tears.

'It's hard,' he said, 'but things are already improving in this village. There's a well now and the kids don't have to walk miles for filthy water. Hope has given them a clinic with a nurse. There's a teacher right here in the village. Things have improved and they can only get better.'

'I know,' she said. 'I know.'

They'd been together for nearly a year. Sometimes Fredrik travelled alone while she stayed in the office, but whenever she could she travelled with him. And if she felt that taking photographs of the suffering seemed intrusive she knew that getting the images out there was what brought attention to the need.

'Come and sit down.' He led her across to a shade tree in the centre of the village and they sat down with their backs to the trunk.

'There'll be ants,' she said.

'No ants, I checked.'

She glanced at him. 'You checked?'

'Absolutely. This is important. Or did you think I'd forget your birthday?'

'It's my birthday?' She'd lost track of the days.

'I'm afraid there are no shops selling pretty birthday cards, nowhere I could buy you the present I had in mind, so one of the ladies here made me this as a place holder, a promise.'

He opened his hand and in his palm lay a small circle of tiny, brightly coloured beads.

'What is it?'

'Give me your hand and I'll show you.' She held out her right hand. 'No, the other one.' He took her left hand in his and holding the bead circle on the tip of her ring finger said, 'There should be diamonds and champagne and there will be, but seeing you here today with these children, I can't wait another moment. Alice Parker, would you do me the greatest honour in the world?

Will you be my wife, my lover, the mother of my children, my partner in everything I do?'

She tried to swallow but her mouth was dry. 'Does that include the mountain rescue bit?' she asked.

'You're already part of that. Your safety PR will stop more than a few idiots getting into trouble.'

'I thought we could raise some funds with one of those calendars with you rescue guys wearing nothing but a bit of rope to cover your embarrassment.'

'If that's what it takes for you to say yes.'

It wasn't the proposal she'd dreamed about as a girl. There were beads instead of diamonds, luke warm water to toast the future instead of champagne but it was a thousand times better than anything she could ever have imagined and she was grinning from ear to ear.

'No conditions, Fredrik Jensson. It's yes. A thousand times yes.'

He slipped the ring on her finger and

she spread her hand to admire it.

'It's beautiful, Fredrik. Perfect. Thank you.' She leaned forward to kiss him, very gently on the lips, and when she drew back she saw that they had an audience of children, all giggling.

'Crack out the cola, chips and cookies, Fredrik. It's my birthday and I'm going to be a countess. We need to party.'

Later, lying together in the darkness of their tent, he said, 'Any thoughts on a wedding? Is the village green calling you?'

'I think the village has had enough fun and I never did have the alpine meadow picnic promised by Prince Carlos.'

'If that's what you want, my darling. That's what you'll have.'

She turned to him. 'All I want is you, Fredrik.'

'I'm yours, my love.' He took the hand bearing his ring and raised it to his lips. 'I'm yours, you are mine and tonight the stars will be shining just a little brighter on our mountain.'

'Ours?' Ally smiled and reached for his hand. 'That's the most beautiful word in the entire world.'

We do hope that you have enjoyed reading this large print book.

Did you know that all of our titles are available for purchase?

We publish a wide range of high quality large print books including:
Romances, Mysteries, Classics
General Fiction
Non Fiction and Westerns

Special interest titles available in large print are:
The Little Oxford Dictionary
Music Book, Song Book
Hymn Book, Service Book

Also available from us courtesy of Oxford University Press:
Young Readers' Dictionary
(large print edition)
Young Readers' Thesaurus
(large print edition)

For further information or a free brochure, please contact us at:
Ulverscroft Large Print Books Ltd.,
The Green, Bradgate Road, Anstey,
Leicester, LE7 7FU, England.
Tel: (00 44) **0116 236 4325**
Fax: (00 44) **0116 234 0205**

Other titles in the
Linford Romance Library:

EMERGENCY NURSE

Phyllis Mallet

Nurse Marion Talbot and Doctor Alan Vincent work together in Casualty. Marion is drawn to him a little more every day — but wonders what she can do to attract his attention. Then they each reveal they will have a relative visiting soon: Marion her mother, and Alan his uncle; and so they hatch a plan to give them a good time, while deciding to meet up themselves. But when a nurse from the hospital is attacked, and the police become involved, things do not run as smoothly as they had anticipated . . .

THE BRIDESMAID'S ROYAL BODYGUARD

After being sacked from her job with a gossip magazine, Ally Parker is given a fresh start when her childhood friend Hope asks her to work PR for her marriage to Prince Jonas of San Michele. When Count Fredrik Jensson, head of security for the royal family, arrives, he makes it clear that Ally's past employment makes her unfit for her role. The fact that there's a sizzle between them from the moment they meet only makes everything worse . . .